HELL'S ANGELS

A Common Smith V.C. story

Germany 1929. England, France and the USA are preparing to de-militarise the West Bank of the Rhine. German nationalists, financed by the great industrialists, have other ideas. They want the area re-incorporated into the Weimar Republic and plan a series of strikes against Allied troops marching westwards. The 'Hell's Angels' – barnstorming German ex-pilots who fled to America after the war – are recalled to Germany for the final attack on the withdrawing allies. Common Smith V.C. and the crew of the *Swordfish* alerted by the mysterious head of the Secret Service, have to stop the Hell's Angels reaching Europe.

HELL'S ANGELS

HELL'S ANGELS

by

Charles Whiting

Magna Large Print Books
Long Preston, North Yorkshire,
BD23 4ND, England.

British Library Cataloguing in Publication Data.

Whiting, Charles
    Hell's angels.

    A catalogue record of this book is
    available from the British Library

    ISBN   0-7505-1906-1

First published in Great Britain 1997
by Severn House Publishers Ltd.

Copyright © 1997 by Charles Whiting

Published in Large Print 2002 by arrangement with
Eskdale Publishing

Magna Large Print is an imprint of Library Magna Books Ltd.

Printed and bound in Great Britain by
T.J. (International) Ltd., Cornwall, PL28 8RW

PART ONE

THE LINE OF WITHDRAWAL 1929

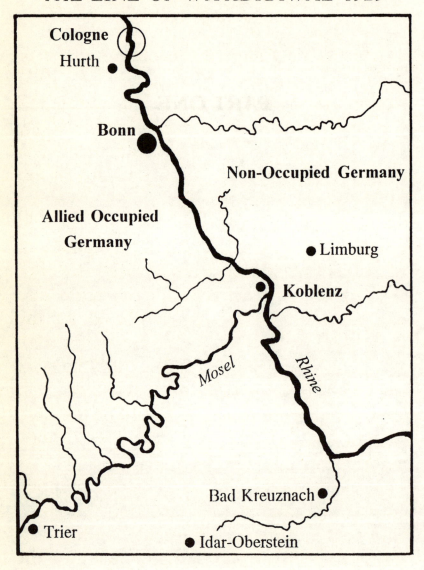

Chapter One

Major McIntyre tensed. His hand gripped the butt of his pistol more tightly. She was moving about now. He could hear her cautious footsteps as she moved out of her hiding place.

Outside there was no sound. Cologne had gone to sleep. On the Rhine, a couple of hundred yards away from the British HQ, the barges had anchored for the night and besides, a thick fog was rolling along the great waterway that linked Germany with the North Sea. He flashed a quick look at the green-glowing dial of his wristwatch. It was just after midnight. It would be the kind of time she would choose to do – he shook his head angrily. *To do what?*

He heard her curse softly as she bumped into something in the darkness. *'Scheisse!'* She said in a decidedly unladylike manner. The officer who had brought her into the HQ four hours before would have been surprised to hear the countess use a word like 'shit'. But then, McIntyre told himself, he had been long asleep, snoring alone in his bed, drunk or drugged, or perhaps both. For he knew that the countess was 'a coke-nose', as the Germans called them, addicted since she had been 18 to cocaine. That was why she was carrying out this potentially dangerous mission, whatever it was.

She had ceased moving now, presumably having found what she had been looking for at the British HQ of the Army of Occupation. McIntyre decided it was time to investigate. He'd catch her red-handed. Almost noiselessly for such a big man, the Canadian major with a face that looked as if it had been sculpted in granite moved forward, his hand gripping the butt of his pistol.

Out of the fog-shrouded river a ship's siren sounded mournfully like the cry of some lost sea creature. He felt a cold finger of fear trace its way down his spine. It was like the old days in the last show when they had been out in no man's land trying to snatch a Hun prisoner when the first star shells had zipped into the sky and they had frozen, knowing that the balloon was about to go up.

Still he moved forward on tiptoe, trying as he did to interpret the odd clicking noise that was coming from her direction. He turned the corner of the corridor. Suddenly his eyes were assailed by a series of bright white flashes. Obviously the countess was using a camera, but to photograph what? He moved on, blinking every time the bright white light flashed.

He halted. Standing at the door, crouching slightly, hand holding his pistol tightly, he watched as the beautiful German woman, her blonde hair tumbling about her face, clicked the shutter of her camera. She appeared to be copying something spread out on the big baize table in front of her. McIntyre strained his eyes and tried to make out what it was. It was a map, but of what he couldn't tell.

The time had come for action. He cleared his throat quite deliberately and said in his best German, *'Guten Abend, Grafin ... was machen Sie hier?'* 'Good evening, Countess. What are you doing here?'

She turned, her face white with shock, her green eyes wide and startled as she saw the big Canadian, his uniform crumpled and untidy as usual but with the big pistol in his hand. 'I ... I...' She stuttered and then collecting herself added, 'I got lost.'

'With a camera in your hand?' he sneered, still speaking German, not taking his eyes off her beautiful face for a moment, for he knew her features would reveal anything she might think of doing. But they remained as they had been, fearful and apprehensive.

He moved forward, jerking the muzzle of his pistol at her to indicate that she had to remain where she was, and flung a glance at the object she had been copying. The lettering at the top told him all he wanted to know, for the time being: *'For General Staff Eyes Only'*. Below there was a map of the west bank of the Rhine with carefully traced routes in red, green and blue leading to Belgium and France. It was obviously a most secret document. She followed the direction of his gaze and quavered, 'I'll do anything you want.' She licked her pink little tongue around her lips suggestively, *'Anything!* But don't give me away!'

He laughed harshly. 'I think you've been doing enough as it is this night, Countess. I guess that young captain got more than his share of it.' He laughed again in that tough, cynical manner of his.

'It doesn't matter. You're a real man,' she stammered. 'He was just a boy.' She hesitated for an instant, then tugged up the skirt of her silk evening dress, slowly and deliberately, revealing the black silk garters, the

12

expanse of white flesh beyond and the fact that she wore no knickers, hoping that he would let her go. She wet her middle finger and drew it through the slight blonde thatch to expose a line of delicate pink flesh. 'Yours for the asking,' she said and looked at him challengingly.

He laughed. 'No thank you, sister,' he said brutally. ''Fraid I might get leprosy or something!' His voice hardened and he snapped in English, which he knew she spoke fluently, 'OK, what's your game? Why are you photographing that map and who in Sam Hill's name are you working for, Countess?'

She let go of the hem of her skirt as if it was red hot, and as it fell to the ground her delightful charms disappeared from view. Her face flushed angrily and she shook her head. 'Do what you wish. I'm not talking to you!'

'Are you sure?'

'Yes.'

He didn't hesitate. With his free hand he lashed out to strike her hard across her beautiful face. She staggered back with a cry of pain. 'You bastard!' she stammered.

'Yes, I know I am,' he said quite calmly, not even breathing hard. 'And there's more of that to come if you don't start talking soon.'

She dabbed her eyes as if to prevent herself from crying. Then she pouted her lips stubbornly, shrugged and said defiantly, 'Keep on trying. You won't get anything out of me, Major McIntyre!'

His eyes lit up. 'You know my name!' he exclaimed. 'You see, you've told me something already, Countess.'

She looked at him, puzzled. 'What?'

'There's only a handful of special people around this headquarters who know my name and line of business. So you've got that knowledge from someone *special*.' He leaned across and then twitched the nipple of her left breast so hard that she whimpered with pain. 'Who is that person?' he rasped.

'I'm not speaking,' she gasped, her beautiful face white with pain.

'Is that so?' McIntyre said calmly. 'Then you've got another think coming, lady.'

She said nothing, so he said, 'We have some Indian soldiers here at HQ. They never get to see a woman. You German girls don't like 'em. Do you know what they would do if I managed to find them a woman – *any woman?*'

He let the words sink in before adding. 'Unfortunately, due to the lack of women, the Indians have developed some unpleasant sexual habits. They have begun to fornicate among themselves.' He shrugged. 'After all they are young men. They have to have some relief.'

She looked at him aghast.

'Yes,' he added as if it was just a fact of life. 'They have commenced buggering each other–'

'Bugger?'

He made an explicit gesture and she shuddered. 'Oh my God!' she quavered. 'Not that!'

'I'm afraid so. They take a great deal of pleasure in that kind of sexual intercourse. Their officers say that that's the only way they can do it these days. They've got so used to the – er – arse.'

She shuddered again, her breasts trembling beneath the sheer silk of her evening gown.

'So,' he concluded. 'If you won't play ball with me, I can't–'

'Von Horn,' she interrupted rapidly.

The Canadian's craggy face lit up instantly. *'Kapitan-leutnant* Von Horn of German Naval Intelligence?'*

*See Charles Whiting, *The Baltic Run*

She nodded urgently.

'Is he behind this business with the secret papers?'

'Yes.'

He whistled softly and then said, 'What's the deal?'

She shrugged and those splendid full breasts of hers, the nipples big and erect, shot temptingly up and down beneath the sheer silk. 'I don't know. Honestly!'

He hesitated for a moment before saying, 'How do you mean you don't know? He must have briefed you somehow or other.'

She looked at him as if he was an idiot. 'You know my problem, I suppose,' she said. 'People like me live for one thing only.' She sniffed hard, as if she were taking cocaine up her nostrils. 'We don't ask questions. As long as they give us the white stuff, that's the only thing which is important.'

He considered her answer for a few moments. Outside on the Rhine the sirens moaned once more. Somewhere an impatient driver was cranking his car moaning, 'For God's sake start up, will you, you bastard!'

McIntyre thought for a few moments, before asking, 'Are you sure you know nothing else? I can make it a lot easier for you if you help me on this?'

'How do you mean?'

'Well, I could have you arrested as a spy which you are, of course. They would send you to prison for that, and,' he paused significantly, 'there would be none of the white stuff behind bars.'

'I'd die,' she said, voice very shaky.

'I doubt it. But you'd have one helluva hard time until you managed to cope. All right, what's it going to be?'

Her beautiful face wrinkled in a worried frown, as she tried to recall what the spymaster von Horn had told her when he had recruited her for this mission. Then she had it. 'I don't know if this means much,' she said hesitantly.

'Go on,' he urged. Outside, the unknown driver had got his car to start and its engine throbbed noisily in the still, pre-dawn air.

'He mentioned something called the "Hell's Angels", something to do with America,' she added. 'I know that because he had a telephone call while I was with him and he said, *die sind doch halb Amis.*''

'They're half Americans anyway,' he translated her words aloud, his tough, hard face, puzzled. 'And that's it, eh?'

'Yes, yes! That's all I do know, honestly!'

McIntyre knew she wasn't lying. Ever since he had been attached to British Intelligence he had carried out enough interrogations these last years to know when the suspect had nothing more to give. 'I believe you,' he said. 'All right, put the camera down on that chair and hitch up your skirts again.' Already he was fumbling with the flies of his breeches.

She didn't hesitate. 'Where?'

'Across the table and let's get it over with quick. I don't want anyone walking in on us in,' he chuckled brutally, 'a compromising position. And I'll see you get some of the white stuff as well.'

A few minutes later it was all over and, panting a little, the big Canadian was reaching into his wallet to pay her. He pulled out a big white £5 note and handed it to her. 'There you are. It was a good fuck. That should buy you a snort of the white stuff.'

She grabbed it with a hand that trembled badly. 'Thanks,' she said and then, to his complete surprise, she reached across and kissed his cheek lightly.

Then she was gone, creeping down the steps towards the exit of the 'Dom Hotel,' which now housed the British HQ, while McIntyre stood there deep in thought. He

18

knew he should call the duty officer to secure the map room which the Countess had entered by stealing the key off her drunken boyfriend. But, before he started to get things moving, he wanted to firm up the little he knew in his mind.

Von Horn, the sinister and ruthless German spymaster, was behind the break-in. So that meant whatever she had been looking for on the secret map of the Rhineland was very important. But what was he to make of these 'Hell's Angels' who were 'half Yanks'? McIntyre cursed, one thing he did know – he would report this back to 'C' in London. If von Horn was involved, the head of the British Secret Intelligence Service had to know.

It was then that it happened. A sudden burst of engine noise, a squeal of protesting rubber. A scream. A crash and an unknown car was speeding away heading for the Hohenzollern Bridge across the Rhine and unoccupied Germany.

McIntyre knew instinctively that the girl was involved. He sprang down the steps two at a time, already drawing and cocking his pistol. But it was too late. In a pool of light cast by the street lamp, she lay sprawled in the careless fashion of violent death. The light from the gas lamp was poor, but he knew she was dead before he reached her. Von Horn had planned this all along. Even if she had succeeded in obtaining the photos of the map, he would have had her eliminated like this. It was his style.

He bent down and turned her round quite gently for a man of his type. She was dead, there was no mistaking that. The car had caught her in the chest. Her breasts were hanging out of the torn gown, squashed, a blood-red gore.

Instinctively, as if he were back on a 'show' in the old war, he pressed her eyelids closed. 'Poor bitch,' he muttered to himself and, rising, started to walk slowly and thoughtfully back to the 'Dom.'

Chapter Two

There was once an old man of Leeds,' one of the grooms was chanting solemnly as they slumped there in the grass waiting for the first chukka to commence, *'Who swallowed a packet of seeds. Great tufts of grass stuck out of his arse ... and his cock was covered in weeds.'*

Dickie Bird grinned at the words and whispered to his old friend and shipmate Common Smith VC, 'Hope the jolly old Admiral doesn't hear that!' He indicated the somewhat portly Admiral Sinclair, Head of the SIS, who was being helped onto his horse with some difficulty, for the beast was very frisky. 'He'll have the poor devil keel-hauled if he does.'

Common Smith chuckled and dabbed his harshly handsome face with his hand-kerchief; it was damnably hot. 'By the looks of things the Admiral is too busy trying to get on that Arab stallion. Christ, it's gone and bit the poor groom again!'

'The thing bites everything, it seems to me,' Bird commented.

Smith nodded a little absently, the glitter-ing spectacle of the polo field with the women in their summer frocks, the ham-pers, the champagne and all the trappings of the British upper class enjoying themselves, forgotten for a few moments.

'Penny for 'em?' Dickie Bird said, seeing the look on his companion's face.

'I was just wondering why the old man called us here. There's this bad business out in Egypt. They're rioting again at Alex. Thought we might have a crack at that.' His frown deepened. 'Doesn't seem to be the case though. Looks like Europe again.'

'Yes. But nothing's happening in Europe at the moment. Even the dashed Huns are quiet for a change now that they're earning the old filthy lucre once more.'

'Agreed, old house,' Smith said. 'That's why I'm puzzled be–'

Dickie Bird nudged him and said out of the side of his mouth, 'See the way that blonde deb is sitting with her legs spread. You can see she isn't a real blonde.'

'Oh, do shut up, Dickie!' Smith said. 'You do rabbit on about women all the time.'

'Only little pleasure your sailor gets, Smithie,' the other man said cheerfully. Then his mouth dropped open suddenly as he followed the direction of Common Smith's gaze. 'As I love and breathe!'

'Exactly,' Smith said. 'There's no mistaking him.'

'There certainly isn't,' the other man agreed, as he took his eyes off the debutante's dark thatch. 'It's trouble personified.'

It was indeed. Approaching them, swaying a little as if he might have had too much to drink, was the familiar figure of Major McIntyre, clad in a thick tweed suit despite the heat, the bulge in his right-hand pocket indicating that as always, contrary to regulations, he was carrying a pistol.

Hastily, the two men rose to their feet. The big Canadian was not a man to be trifled with, especially when he had been drinking, which was most of the time these days. The strain of his job working for 'C' was beginning to tell.

'Hello Mac,' they said as one. 'Hell's Last Issue have returned.' It was a reference to his old regiment, the Highland Light Infantry of Canada.

'Ay, that it has,' he said, the accent of the Gorbals, where he had been born still noticeable under the Canadian twang. He sat down heavily and brought out a silver flask. 'Fancy a snort?' he growled in his no-nonsense fashion.

'Not on the polo field, old chap,' Dickie Bird said indignantly. 'Only champers here, you know!'

'Toffee-nosed twits,' McIntyre said and raising the flask to his lips took a hefty swig.

Common Smith VC waited till he had finished before asking, 'Where's the fire, old chap? What's the problem?'

'The friggin' Huns, that's the problem – as friggin' always,' the Canadian growled back. 'They've bin a friggin' problem ever since I

23

can remember. I think they'll be one long after I've gone.'

'Is that why you're here–' Common Smith began, but the shrill whistle to start the chukka interrupted him and he turned to look at the field, as Admiral Sinclair swung his polo stick and set off after the opposition, who were tearing down the field at a tremendous pace.

'Good God Almighty!' McIntyre exclaimed in wonder, 'What's the Old Man doing on that horse? Is he gonna kill himself?'

The Arab stallion was galloping after the opposition, yellow teeth bared, snapping angrily as it got closer to the nearest horse. The other player, seemingly unaware that the stallion was after him, gave a backhand. But to do so, he paused slightly. It was a fatal move. The stallion leaned forward and sank its teeth into the white breeches of the opposition player. The latter yelled with pain. Caught by surprise, his mount trod on the ball which became embedded in the turf.

Desperately, the portly Admiral took a swing at the polo ball. He missed. Instead, his polo stick swept under the other horse's tail. The mare, obviously very sensitive about such matters, slammed its tail to its rear to block any further advances on its

24

maidenly charms and the Admiral's stick was imprisoned.

Together the Admiral and the other player galloped, locked together, past the Prince of Wales's box, with the crowd laughing uproariously at the spectacle until finally the umpire blew his whistle and the dreadful chukka was over at last.

Admiral Sinclair limped up to them, panting hard and dabbing his pudgy face with a silk handkerchief as they rose to their feet to welcome their chief. 'What a damned shambles!' he panted. 'Can't show my face on a polo field for a damned long time, I can assure you of that.'

Dickie Bird pulled himself together with considerable difficulty. 'Bit of bad luck, sir,' he commented.

'Bad luck! That's not the bloody word for it,' Sinclair snapped, looking at the young officer as if wondering whether his leg was being pulled. In the end he decided that it wasn't and said, 'Come over to my Roller. My chap has got some champers on ice. Fancy a spot of it at this moment? Besides, I want to talk to the three of you.'

Common Smith looked at the embarrassed Admiral keenly. 'A mission for *Swordfish*, sir?' he asked, referring to his boat.

'Perhaps. All a bit confused at the moment. McIntyre here can tell you more. Come on chaps!'

With the Admiral in the lead, trailing his polo stick through the grass as if it weighed a ton, they walked over to the ancient Rolls Royce where a smart-looking servant waited for him, keen eyes taking in everything and with a bulge in his right pocket which indicated that he, too, was carrying a firearm.

'Jenkins, get out the bloody champers – and double quick time!'

'Sir,' the servant answered instantly with the alacrity of a naval petty officer, which he had been before the Germans had blown off his right leg at the Battle of Jutland back in '16.

As soon as the ice-cold champagne was served, the servant moved away, hand in his right pocket as if he expected trouble at any moment, while the Admiral began his briefing. 'The Army is leaving Germany – in fact all three of the occupying powers are withdrawing from the Rhineland. For the time being the whole thing is highly secret, but it's going to be done.'

'Be nice to the Hun!' McIntyre sneered.

'Something like that,' the Admiral agreed, not looking up as the grooms led away the

Arab stallion which had caused him so much trouble. 'It's also a cost-cutting exercise.' He looked up as the stallion was pushed into its box and began lashing out at the woodwork. 'Nasty beast,' he commented, 'Hope he breaks a damned leg and they have to put the bugger down. Now then,' his voice rose, 'the question is what will happen when we, the French and the Yanks leave?' He answered his own question after a moment. 'Officially – *nothing*. I have been informed that the German authorities will not attempt to send in troops. The Rhineland west of the River Rhine will remain de-militarized, which is what we want.' He shrugged and took another drink of the sparkling wine. 'However, there are those in Germany who will not be content with that situation.' He nodded to the Canadian.

Hurriedly, his craggy face sullen, as if he were angry at the whole world, McIntyre told the other two what had happened at the British Army headquarters in Cologne the previous week.

'So the girl,' the Admiral summed it up for them, 'was obviously attempting to get a copy of the routes through which we will evacuate our troops to Belgium when the time comes to leave the Rhineland.'

'But why, sir?' Common Smith asked.

Sinclair frowned. 'Ay, there's the rub,' he said. 'Why?'

'Could this von Horn chappie be trying to sabotage the evacuation of our troops, sir?' Dickie Bird suggested, as the stallion lashed its hooves against the woodwork of the box in impotent fury.

'Why?' Sinclair asked. 'After all, he and the other nationalists like that crazy man Hitler and the rest want to get shot of us. What good would it do them trying to prevent us from leaving?'

They fell silent. The only sound now was that of popping champagne corks and the battering the wild stallion was giving the horsebox. Already the woodwork was beginning to splinter.

'The dead Hun said something about "Hell's Angels" and half Americans,' McIntyre volunteered after a while.

'Hell's Angels,' Dickie Bird repeated the name thoughtfully, 'Isn't that the name they gave to the Flying Corps in the last show?'

Common Smith shook his head. 'No, not to our chaps, Dickie, but to the Huns – the pilots of von Richthofen's squadron. You know, the legendary Red Baron that they're always going on about.'

Admiral Sinclair looked up, slightly startled. 'What did you say, Smith?'

Common Smith repeated his statement.

Sinclair whistled softly. 'I know what you mean, Smith. But officially the new Germany is not allowed to have an air force under the terms of the Treaty of Versailles.'

McIntyre laughed scornfully. *'Officially,* there are a lot of things the old Hun is not allowed to possess, but that doesn't mean he hasn't got them. Planes manufactured in Switzerland and Russia. Subs and tanks in Sweden. Oh, yes, they've got the goods if they need them!'

'Still,' Sinclair said sternly, 'that doesn't explain these Hell's Angels and the half-Yankee bit, Major.'

McIntyre muttered something but didn't answer.

'So where do we come in, sir?' Smith asked eagerly, for the *Swordfish* and her crew had been beached in the wilds of East Yorkshire for too long now and all of them were growing restless. Action, any kind of action, was what they needed now.

By way of an answer, the portly Admiral drew a line in the bare patch of ground in front of him with the handle of his polo stick. 'The German border rivers – Moselle

– here, then the Sauer and Our – here and here. They separate Germany from France, Luxembourg and Belgium and the three occupying powers will be pulling back in due course across those rivers. Once they're clear of that, er, damned Hun Fatherland, that will be that. Now I feel there is a need for our service to, among other things, patrol those rivers until the withdrawal commences.' He looked hard at Common Smith. 'That's where you and the crew of the *Swordfish* come in. Your craft has a very shallow draught so I think you'll be all right on them, though I think the Our, the most northern of the rivers, will be too much for even the *Swordfish*.'

Smith nodded his understanding and said in a slightly puzzled tone, 'But what would we be looking for, sir? What do you think the Huns might do?'

Now it was Sinclair's turn to look puzzled. 'To be frank, Common Smith, I don't quite know. But if their right-wing lunatics are going to strike it's going to be while we're pulling back. In that way they would achieve the maximum publicity. So what can I say? Be on your guard for anything untoward, like suspicious characters at the bridges we're going to use to cross into Allied countries.'

'Bit of a tall order, sir,' Dickie Bird said in that languid manner of his, while McIntyre stared at the circle of light far off, winking in the sun, wondering what it could be.

'I know,' Sinclair agreed. 'But you chaps have been at this game since 1918. You know the form. I'm sure you'll do your best.' He looked at the two young former naval officers and told himself that they were the best Old England could produce. As long as the public schools kept turning out young men like the two of them the Empire was safe. He finished off the rest of his champers and rose heavily to his feet in the same instant that the one-legged ex-petty officer came back to the ancient Rolls Royce, stood to attention and said out of the side of his mouth, 'We're being watched, sir.'

Chapter Three

Kapitanleutnant von Horn took off his cap to reveal his cropped yellow hair cut so close to his scalp that it looked as if he were wearing a yellow skullcap. He looked at his captive with eyes that were the pale blue of a glacier.

It was the face of a cold-blooded murderer, she knew that already. She shuddered.

As if in some kind of ritual he then took the cheroot from beneath his thin slits of lips and ground it out slowly and deliberately in the ashtray on the pale wooden board table of the cell in which they had imprisoned her. Again she shuddered, half suspecting what was to come.

In the shadows, the man they code-named 'Wolf', threateningly slapped his dog-whip against his boot, revealing his impatience with the whole business, for he had to fly back to Munich this day. There were things to be done, now that he had decided he would make another attempt to take over power from the hated Weimar Government, filled with traitors who had stabbed Germany in the back in 1918.

'Well?' von Horn demanded. 'What can you tell me, wench, eh? When are the Tommies going to begin their move?'

'I've tried my best,' she quavered, tears in her eyes once more. For the hulking petty officer who stood behind her chair had already knocked her about as soon as they had taken her from the Berlin train and brought her here to the naval barracks, von Horn's HQ.

'It's not good enough,' von Horn said, peering at her in the poor light of the single naked bulb. 'You were employed to find out the information and you apparently have failed. There has to be punishment for that, you know.'

In the shadows, the man they code-named 'Wolf', said in his thick, guttural Austrian accent, 'Please get on with it, *Herr Kapitan-leutnant*. I haven't got all the time in the world. Use any method you like, *I* won't object.'

'Yessir,' von Horn replied. He turned his attention back to the terrified girl, who clutched her ripped blouse with skinny hands as if she expected the big, brutal petty officer, breathing down her neck, to tear it off her at any moment. 'Come on! Out with it! What did this pig of an Englishman say? After all you did spread your legs for the filthy swine. He owed you something, didn't he?'

It had been her job to ply the troop train carrying the officers of the Allied Control Commission from Cologne to Berlin. Her cover was that of a stewardess; in fact she was a prostitute who serviced high-ranking officers in their private compartments and sometimes in Berlin's Hotel Esplanade if von Horn thought they could be pumped for more information. It was a rough, tough life. Some of the officers she slept with had been brutalized by four years in the trenches or hated the 'Huns', as they always called the Germans, with such passion that they didn't care about what swinish indignities they inflicted upon her.

Then she had met General Richardson, 'Richie of the Cherrypickers', as he was known to his contemporaries.* He had been different, kind and understanding and a bit lonely. His wife had divorced him and his only son had been killed in action. He had become more like a father to her than a lover. ''Fraid the spirit is willing, m'dear,' he had often proclaimed when they had stayed together at the Esplanade, 'but the jolly old flesh is a bit weak, y'know!'

Once he had said to her in his hearty, though gentle manner, 'I know you're a whore m'girl, but I like you. If you could see your way to it, you could come and live with me when I retire. Naturally we couldn't go back to the old country. Scandal and all that. But on my pension I think we could

*The 11th Hussars, known as 'Cherry-pickers' on account of their scarlet trousers.

34

live quite nicely together in Monte, and the climate's better there anyway.'

She had reported that conversation to von Horn as she was obliged to if she wanted to keep working the Allied trains and had regretted it ever since. For the albino with the cruel eyes had assumed she had a special hold on the ageing general and had made her pump him for information. Unfortunately 'Richie of the Cherrypickers' had not been much interested any more in military matters. 'Bin at it now since the Sudan,' he would often remark, nursing the weak whisky which was all he allowed himself in the way of drink these days. 'Done my bit. Just waiting for my pension to come through so I can get into mufti.'

Von Horn had not accepted the fact. Time and time again he had pressed her to pump the General for information and time and time she had protested that he had little to give. As he insisted, 'Just an office Johnny these days. Let my batman put up my medals and polish my boots and I wander around Berlin with my sword dangling trying to look important,' and he would guffaw in that horsey fashion of his displaying his yellowing false teeth. And then she had felt something akin to love for him, for he was simply an old man waiting to die.

Now she stared up at von Horn fearfully and waited for the interrogation to begin and she had no doubts about how it would end if she didn't come up with something for him. Von Horn was a sadist, he loved inflicting pain and wouldn't hesitate to do so.

In the shadows, the civilian they called 'Wolf' slapped his riding boot once more with his dog-whip, his impatience all too clear. Von Horn noted the sound and rasped, 'Listen wench, this is what I want to know. Does the English swine know anything about *when* they are going to evacuate the Rhineland? A simple question which requires a simple answer.' He looked significantly at the big, burly petty officer and she knew what the look meant. If she didn't come up with something, they would beat her again. It wouldn't be the first time.

Desperately she racked her brains. Mostly the General talked about the past, or, when he was in the mood, which wasn't very often now, about sex. He rarely mentioned military matters. 'Too long in the tooth, m'dear,' he'd say. 'Leave it to the other chaps who want to get on. Nobody tells me much anyway. They knew my days are numbered. Once they go from Germany I shall hand in my papers.'

'Well?' von Horn demanded.

Behind her the petty officer jerked so hard at her hair that tears of pain sprang into her eyes. She gasped and von Horn said, 'There will be worse than that soon, if you don't come up with something.'

In the shadows 'Wolf' cleared his throat, very irritated with all the delay.

She sobbed, 'I remember the General saying he would retire when the British leave the Rhineland, but didn't say when that would be.'

'Say that again!' von Horn snapped eagerly.

She repeated her statement and von Horn stalked across the cell to 'Wolf' and whispered, 'That's a clue, Wolf.'

'How do you mean?'

Von Horn lowered his voice even more so that the whore couldn't hear. 'The Tommies are a very pedantic people. Unlike us they can't hand in their papers at any time and quit their regiment. It has to be done at fixed times, every quarter in other words. So the next quarter commences on the first of September 1929. That would fit in with what we have already heard of their evacuation of the Rhineland.'

'I see. So that would give us two weeks to

finalize our plans,' Wolf said.

'Yes.'

'I could get my people organized in the Ruhr and Rhineland by then and prepare for the revolt to come. But what about the chaps in America you mentioned to me before. It takes about four to five days to get from that country to Europe by boat, doesn't it?'

'Yes. But if your party can raise the money immediately we can hire a small steamer to bring them across with their gear,' Von Horn made a quick calculation. 'They could be in Germany, ready for action, in eight to nine days. It will be nip and tuck but it can be done, providing we get the money at once.'

'You shall have the money. There are many powerful and rich people backing the Party now. They would be glad to help us in the sacred cause of re-uniting our beloved Fatherland.' The Austrian spoke with calm determination like a man who knew he was in complete charge of the situation. 'Good!' he concluded. 'I shall now drive to Hamburg-Funlsbuttel and take the midday plane to Munich. I will telephone you about the money tonight.'

'Thank you,' von Horn said, as the man code-named 'Wolf' stepped out of the shadows and as was customary in his new Party, raised his right hand in salute, barking *'Heil!'*

Automatically von Horn did the same, clicking to attention and using the 'German greeting' himself, *'Heil Hitler!'*

The whore looked startled and it was clear from the look in her eyes that she knew who 'Wolf' was, too. Von Horn frowned as did Adolf Hitler. 'What will you do with her?' he asked and then added hastily, 'Perhaps it is better I do not know.'

Von Horn nodded his agreement as the whore blanched with fear. Moments later Hitler had entered the waiting car which would take him to nearby Hamburg.

Von Horn waited till the car had drawn away, then he nodded to the big petty officer. 'All right, *Obermaat,* you know what to do?'

'Jawohl Herr Kapitanleutnant,' the man replied dutifully. 'Up, bitch – on your feet,' he growled, 'you're going for a little walk with me.' He grinned at her evilly.

They went out, leaving von Horn with his thoughts and ignoring the whimpering pleas of the Tommy whore who had guessed what was in store for her. His brain raced. At last, after ten years, Germany would be able to take charge of its own destiny once more.

One decisive blow, the rallying cry for the whole nation, would sweep away those socialists and office-seekers who had betrayed Imperial Germany back in 1918. The re-occupation of the Rhineland, west of Germany's great river, would be the signal. Then the Fatherland could resume its holy mission of recreating its Empire. He relit his black cheroot and leaned back in his chair, telling himself he would have a boy this night, to celebrate, cost what it may. For soon there would be no time for such delights. For a few moments he allowed himself the luxury of lusting after pretty boys with rouged lips and plucked eyebrows ogling him in the ill-lit backstreets where the 'pavement pounders', as they were nicknamed, plied their trade.

Suddenly his reverie was disturbed by a shriek of pain and the sound of a body falling to the ground. He rose hastily and hurried down the corridor which led from the torture cell to the first floor of Naval Intelligence HQ and flung open the door.

In the yard the burly petty officer was writhing back and forth on the ground in total agony, his knees raised, his hands clutching his genitals, vomit trickling out of the side of his gaping mouth.

'What in three devils' names has happened, *Obermaat?*' von Horn demanded, flinging away his cheroot angrily, 'Come on, man, *out with it!*'

'She grabbed my, my cock, sir,' the petty officer said thickly, 'and pulled it. When I let go of the bitch she went and kneed me, the whore!'

'You mean – *she's gone?*' von Horn cried in alarm.

But he received no answer from the pain-stricken petty officer, who was too busy being sick again.

Hastily von Horn surveyed the yard and the street beyond. But both were empty save for a yellow-painted tram, its bell ringing gaily, disappearing up the street; and von Horn didn't need a crystal ball to know who was on it, – *the whore.*

Chapter Four

'Shell-shock,' Dickie Bird said, 'Poor devil.'

They were standing outside York's great Victorian pile, the 'Station Hotel', enjoying the weak September sunshine and staring at the city's ancient walls, waiting for the train to Hull to come in. From there they would travel to the remote East Yorkshire port of Withernsea – 'the arsehole of the world,' as the crew of the Swordfish called their secret base – from whence they would set out on their new mission.

The middle-aged man was clad very formally in a black jacket, striped trousers and wearing a bowler and carrying a furled umbrella over his right arm. Obviously he had once been an officer, judging by the cut of it. Now he slammed his right foot down in front of the letterbox bearing the legend 'G V R', as if he were on a parade ground, and bellowed, 'General salute – present ... *present arms.*'

Then using the umbrella he went through the intricate ritual of saluting the letterbox with the royal insignia as if he were saluting the king-emperor.

A few passing schoolchildren giggled and laughed at the sight. But most of the onlookers looked sad. The Great War had produced too many harmless lunatics such as the man saluting: men who had not been able to stand up to the horrors of the trenches and had cracked.

The man in the bowler hat stamped his

foot down once more and cried, as if addressing a whole battalion of infantry on parade, 'Slope arms! Order arms!' He went through the motions with his stick and then bellowed, 'Stand at ease ... *stand easy.*' Again he went through the motions and stood there, feet set apart at the regulation angle, stick resting at the side of his leg as if it were a rifle.

'Funny,' Common Smith said, a little puzzled.

'I wouldn't call him funny,' Dickie Bird said idly, knowing that his old shipmate was not normally hurtful or cruel.

'No, I didn't mean the poor devil's performance,' Common Smith said hastily. 'I feel sorry for him.'

'What then?'

'Well,' the other man said hesitantly, 'look at the way he's dressed.'

'What about it?'

'Well, it's correct in every detail. Just the way an officer would dress in mufti when off duty, except for one thing.'

'And what's that?'

'He's wearing brown boots – very shabby brown boots. Just look how worn they are! No self-respecting ex-officer would wear brown boots with a dark suit. You know how

fussy the brown jobs' – he meant soldiers –
'are.'

'Yes, I see what you mean. But after all,
Smithie, the man is bonkers. Perhaps he just
forgot–' He stopped short. The shell-
shocked man was crying. 'Parade will retire,
about turn!' in that same instant turning to
face them, then he was bringing up the stick
and pointing it directly at the two friends as
if it were a rifle.

Dickie Bird could see that the man was as
crazy as a loon. But there was a kind of mad
purpose in his eyes as he squinted along the
stock of the stick.

'I say, Smithie, what's he up to–'

Smith didn't answer. Instead he gave his
friend a great shove with his left shoulder
just as a soft pop and faint wisp of smoke
appeared at the end of the stick. Dickie Bird
fell to his knees crying, 'Hey, what's the
damned game!' But behind him, a fat
woman, carrying a shopping basket,
screamed, shrill and hysterical. She went
reeling back, her left eye shattered and filled
with blood.

Things happened swiftly. A great, green
Lagonda appeared from nowhere. Just as
Smith dashed forward to grapple with the
man with the stick, the car squealed to a

44

halt. Hands reached out and grabbed the man and dragged him inside, his stick falling from his hand, and roared away with the door half open. Moments later it had disappeared over the hill which led from York station. It had all happened so suddenly that the two friends could hardly believe it had occurred at all.

But behind them the woman dying on the pavement, lying in a bright red pool of her own blood, told them it had.

But why had the 'shell-shocked' civilian fired upon them and who had grabbed him in the car and hauled him away at such speed?

'We've been onto Special Branch in London,' the tall, heavy-set local police inspector reported as they sat deep in thought in the bar of the 'Station Hotel' sipping at their whisky as the light started to go outside and they waited for further orders. 'We are to drive you under escort to Withernsea to where your craft is. London has told us you're not to take any further chances?'

Common Smith nodded his understanding and asked, still subdued by the strange events of the afternoon, 'Anything new?'

'A bit, sir.' The inspector brushed back his thick moustache, as if to ensure that it was still there. 'We know the chap who shot at you. Well, we know a bit *about* him. He was an officer with the West Yorks on the Somme in Sixteen. He received a bad head wound, they say he has two silver plates in the back of his skull. At all events, when he recovered they had to send him to Naburn, that's a local lunatic asylum, for a while. But we know that he's not all that touched. People think he's barmy, but he also works as a bookie's lookout. He's always there whenever the local bobbies start trying to catch a bookie out. He signals in that crazy fashion of his that we're on the way. He likes his booze and brass – and he'd do anything for either.'

'Well. Who paid him, Inspector?' Dickie Bird asked.

'Don't know that yet exactly, sir,' the Inspector replied promptly. 'But we do know that the Lagonda was hired in Leeds, and it was hired by two foreign gentlemen.'

'Foreign?' the two listeners said as one.

The inspector nodded. 'Something else. The garage owner who rented it to them in Leeds is of the Jewish persuasion.'

At other times the two would have laughed

at such officialese, but not now. They were too intrigued.

'Well, he says he speaks something called Yiddish. It must be a sort of Jewish, I suppose, and he says that Yiddish is a bit like German.' The inspector hesitated for a moment, his face set in a puzzled frown, as if it was very confusing to him. Smith could understand his position. In a provincial city like York, his 'cases' would be naughty boys riding cycles after dark without lights, kids 'scrumping' apples, or perhaps tramps begging for a halfpenny in the streets. Now he was dealing with a murder, perhaps for the first time in his career. 'Well the two men who hired the car spoke German.'

'Oh, my sainted aunt!' Dickie Bird exclaimed and nearly choked on his drink.

'So they're on to us already,' Common Smith said grimly.

'Don't know about that, sir,' the inspector said respectfully, for, as had most of the country, he had heard all about Smith, who gained his VC when barely out of his teens and when asked by a reporter what his title was as the son of the Earl of Beverly had replied, 'I'm just common Smith.'*

*See Charles Whiting, *The Baltic Run*

'Oh and there's one more thing,' added the inspector. 'You are to call this number in London as soon as I'm finished. We'll use the telephone kiosk in the hall. Mr Bird and myself are to guard the kiosk while you make the telephone call. Those are my strict orders.' He handed Smith a folded slip of paper. 'And when you've done so you're to destroy the paper with the number on it. Again, orders, sir.'

Hastily Smith unfolded the slip and looked at the number. It was 'C's' the Head of Intelligence. He nodded at Dickie, who had already guessed who they were to call, and they rose immediately. 'C' did not tolerate tardiness.

All three of them went to the kiosk in the foyer and when the inspector and Dickie Bird had posted themselves outside the box, Smith asked the operator to connect him with 'C's London Number.

It took some time and while Smith waited he visualized the innocent-looking house in Queen Anne's Gate which housed the Secret Intelligence Service. Already he knew 'C's aides would be vetting the call. Many of them were regular officers from traditional regiments with deceptively charming manners. But they were tough, men who had carried out covert operations from the Hindu Kush right across the world to Mexico.

'Yes,' the voice snapped without any further introduction, but then Smith needed none. He recognized it immediately for it still carried the hard decisiveness of the quarter-deck when Sinclair had been a fighting sailor.

'I was asked to call, sir,' Smith said, not giving his name either.

'Good! I have some news for you. Canuck' – the Admiral meant McIntyre – 'has gone over the wire.'

Smith gasped. He knew what that meant. The tough Canadian intelligence agent had ventured into unoccupied Germany on the other side of the Rhine.

'Bit dicey, sir,' he said, keeping his voice under control. He knew that the female operators in York wouldn't get many calls to London. In all probability one of them would be listening in to the conversation and he didn't want to give anything away that they might gossip about later. One couldn't be too careful these days.

'Yes, I understand that,' Admiral Sinclair boomed, 'But you know our tame Canuck. He's not afraid of taking risks, especially

49

when he's got a lead.'

'Has he?'

'Yes, the Hun sailor's definitely behind it and – well, I can't tell you any more over the telephone. I'll keep you informed as soon as the Canuck gets back with the lead. Your task now is to get underway as soon as possible. I'll signal you further instructions when you get to you know where.'

'Yessir.'

'Good show! One thing, young man, don't take the slightest risk. It's obvious from what happened today that the Huns are on to us. No risks – and watch your back!'

'Yessir.'

The phone went dead, leaving Smith to stare at the wall in front of him, his mind racing electrically.

Five minutes later they were hurrying out of York in a police car, with another one containing the inspector following at a respectful distance to ascertain whether or not they were being trailed. Now with their security ensured, Common Smith VC was able to tell Dickie Bird everything he knew.

Bird listened attentively and when Smith was finished said. 'That McIntyre, he really doesn't give a damn, does he!'

'Good man to have on our side,' Common

Smith answered, as they approached Hull. 'We'll find out soon enough what he's discovered. Now our main task is to get *Swordfish* ready for sea and then cross the Channel.'

'There's one small problem there, old bean,' Bird said in his usual flippant fashion, though for once his face was serious. 'I've been thinking about it.'

'What's that, Dickie?'

'In order to get into the Moselle, we'll have to sail the Rhine until we reach Koblenz where the Moselle flows into that river.'

'God, I never thought of that,' Smith said, a little shocked.

'Yes, and if this chap von Horn knows we're coming you can bet your bottom dollar he'll do everything in his power to stop us, Smithie.'

Common Smith nodded grimly, but said nothing as he considered the prospect before them. They drove the rest of the way to Withernsea in stony silence.

Chapter Five

The whore waited in the shadows. She knew that her pursuers would expect her to head for Cologne and the safety offered by the protection of General Richardson. But she had been cautious enough not to take the direct route. Instead she had used her travel pass for the *Reichsbahn* to take local trains from Hamburg, working her way slowly southwards to the Rhine, changing trains frequently. With the money in the wallet taken from the brutal petty officer, who would have killed her if she had not injured him, she bought peasant-style clothes so that travelling third class on the hard wooden seats no one would have taken her for a sophisticated prostitute who was the mistress of a British general.

At Munster she had dared to telephone the General. For a man of his age and mentality he had acted with surprising speed and decision. He had told her that she must stop at Duisburg. The Germans would obviously be watching the Rhine crossing's road and rail, plus the trams across the Rhine into Cologne. She would wait outside the station there, where she would be contacted by one of his agents. He had described the officer in question, adding, 'you'll know him because he speaks English with a Canadian accent.' He'd asked if she heard a Canadian accent before, to which she replied dutifully that she did, but she didn't tell her aged lover that she had heard it a good few times while in bed.

The General had ended the conversation with a reassuring, 'Now, don't worry m'dear. Within twenty-four hours we'll have you out safely. In a month's time we'll be both toasting our toes in the sunshine at Monte, you can rest assured of that.'

The words *had* reassured her. But now as she waited, with time slipping by, she was beginning to lose her confidence once more. It would soon be dark and if she hung around the station for long, the leather-helmeted *schupo* who patrolled the streets outside might well come over and move her along, probably thinking she was some village girl trying to sell her body for extra money. She had had experience enough of that kind of thing in the past. Her stomach was grumbling too and she would have given her soul for a bowl of hot goulash soup and a roll, but she daren't chance going into a third-class buffet to eat. Von Horn might well have his agents waiting in such a place for her; it would be the kind of spot they would choose. So she patrolled the darkening street outside the station, which was now beginning to settle down for the night with fewer and fewer passengers going in and out. And all the time she flashed impatient glances at the big illuminated clock, willing the General's man to appear and take her away to safety.

Time passed with leaden feet. Once, a middle-aged man with a stick and Homburg approached her. He raised his hat politely and said softly, 'Would you like to do me a little favour, Fraulein? Nothing dramatic. If you'd hold it in your hand there's ten marks in it for you. No unpleasantness, I can assure you.'

She started and then caught herself. 'I'm a good girl,' she snapped in what she hoped would be taken for a peasant dialect. 'I'm waiting for my betrothed – to finish his shift,' she added, as if he might make an appearance at any moment.

That did it. Hastily the middle-aged man raised his Homburg to her, saying, 'I'm sorry, I mistook you for a certain type of woman.' He walked away hurriedly, as if he expected her 'betrothed' to appear at any moment. At any other time she would have laughed at the little encounter, but not now; she was too worried.

A little later a fat-bellied *schupo* looked across at her suspiciously. She trembled with fear as he appeared about to come over to her. Then he'd ask her for her identity card. But he changed his mind and sauntered away, hand on his rubber truncheon, obviously thinking she was harmless. She breathed a sigh of heartfelt relief.

It was just about then that a car drove up to come to a halt some 50 metres away on the opposite side of the street. The driver turned off his lights, which seemed strange but then she thought it might be the car of her rescuer. She looked desperately across at it, but neither of the two men in front got out and she told herself they were just waiting for someone to get off the train and be picked up. She sighed in the same instant that a voice from behind her said, 'Fraulein Lena, don't look round. I've been sent to help you.'

He heart skipped a beat. The words were in German, but there was no mistaking that

Canadian accent.

'I'm going to pass you by. Count to sixty and then follow me. Don't try to talk to me. I'm coming now.'

A man in a rough tweed suit, obviously not German-made, strolled slowly past by her. He was fumbling in his pocket as he did so. She started to count off to 60, hoping he wouldn't walk so fast that she might lose him. But he seemed to have all the time in the world, as he stopped for an instant and fumbled in his pocket again to take out a cigarette. He crossed the road, apparently very casually, to where the darkened car was parked. Next to it he stopped again, flicked a match with his thumb nail. There was a spurt of blue flame as the two occupants turned their faces away from the sudden light. The man in the tweed suit didn't seem to notice. Instead he concentrated all his attention, or so it seemed, on lighting his cigarette.

Fifty-nine … sixty,' she counted to herself and walked after him, forcing her trembling legs to go slowly, not wanting to attract any attention to herself. The man in the tweed suit turned the corner. She did the same a few seconds later.

He was waiting for her in the shadows, a

56

tough-looking man with a face which looked as if it had been hewn from granite. Now he spoke in English, and the accent was *definitely* Canadian. He held his finger to his lips for silence, whispering. 'The two men in the car are on the lookout for you. Both belong to that guy Hitler's National Socialist Party. They had the Party buttons in their lapels.'

'He's involved,' she whispered.

'Who?'

'Hitler.'

'Thought he would be. One bad Hun – er, German – that one! Obviously this is gonna be something big. But let's concentrate on getting you out of this mess. They're guarding all bridges across the Rhine. We know that. And they're looking for you.'

She went pale in the yellow light of the gas-lamp close by.

Hastily McIntyre said, 'Don't panic. We're going to get you across. But first we've got to get to the Rhine and shake these guys off.'

'The ones in the car?'

'Yeah, and the other ones. From what we found out this is a max effort show. They've got people everywhere and naturally the cops are working for them as well. They're all supporters of these Nazis. They are members of the German National Socialist Workers' Party.'

She opened her mouth to ask what she should do next when behind them, around the corner, the car engine started up. McIntyre looked grim. He said nothing, but pulled out his pistol and swiftly attached a long, round object to its muzzle. 'Silencer,' he commented laconically, 'just in case. Come on. Take it easy. I've got an automobile up on the waste ground ahead.'

As if they had all the time in the world, although she was quaking with fear for she half guessed what was to come, they strolled along the pavement to the waste ground in the shadows ahead.

Behind them the car approached in low gear, its headlights searching the darkness like a pair of malevolent eyes. He tightened his grip on her arm. 'Don't panic!' he hissed out of the side of his mouth. 'It's gonna be okay.'

Now the car had almost reached them. She felt a cold finger of fear trace its way down her spine. She shivered knowing instinctively it was going to happen, now.

'Hey, *Sie da*,' a harsh voice challenged. '*Bleiben Sie stehen.*'

'Do as they say,' he hissed. 'Stop!'

Her legs felt as if they were going to give way beneath her at any moment. He dug his big fingers into her arm cruelly. She stopped. He turned slowly, outlined in the yellow light of the headlights. *'Ja?'* he enquired, softly for him.

'Wo woollen Sie hin?' the harsh voice asked suspiciously and there was the metallic creak of the nearside door of the car being opened.

'To my car,' McIntyre answered in what he hoped was a humble, slightly scared voice. In the cover of his pocket he gripped the silenced pistol more firmly. In a minute, he told himself, it was going to be piss or get off the friggin' pot.

'Just stay there,' the harsh voice commanded. 'I want to see your papers.' They heard the speaker's feet rasping on the cobbles. He was coming towards them. The girl thrust her fist into her mouth to prevent herself from screaming with fear.

McIntyre tensed and then relaxed, sensing that old feeling of the trenches, that fatalistic coolness that had always overcome him when he'd known the balloon had gone up and there was no turning back. He waited.

The German did what McIntyre hoped he

would do. He walked in front of the car's headlights so that he was perfectly outlined against the twin beams. 'Sucker!' McIntyre sneered contemptuously at the man's lack of expertise. Next moment he pulled the trigger of the silenced pistol. There was a soft plop. The man staggered in mid-pace, clutching his chest in sudden alarm and shock. Blood seeped through his tightly clenched fingers. He stared down at it as if he couldn't believe that this was happening to him. Next moment he pitched face-forward, unconscious or dead before he hit the cobbles.

McIntyre fired again. The window of the car shattered into a glittering spider's web of broken glass. There was a yelp of pain. Suddenly the headlights went out. McIntyre waited no longer. 'Come on!' he cried to the petrified girl, 'Let's run for it!' Clutching her arm with his free hand, he pulled her along with him.

Behind him the car started up again and began to follow the running couple, grinding along in low gear, the driver obviously having difficult in seeing. McIntyre cursed. There was no time for another shootout. He had to use a risky but instant method of knocking out the driver. 'Keep running!' he

60

panted, tugging the little round object from his other pocket. He put it to his lips and pulled out the pin with his teeth. *'One ... two ... three,'* he counted off the seconds and then with all his might, like a baseball pitcher, he flung it at the advancing car.

In spite of the shattered windscreen, the driver must have seen it coming. He swung the steering wheel round violently. Too late! The grenade exploded directly beneath the vehicle's front axle. *Whoosh!* There was a thick crump, followed an instant later by a burst of angry scarlet flame. The front of the car reared into the air. The axle shattered. A wheel cobbled away. Next moment the whole car burst into flames. No one got out.

Then they were running for the little three-wheeler van, piled high with black briquets and bearing the legend, *'Schmitz & Sohne, Kohlenhandler'* on its side. 'In you go,' he panted, pushing her in by her delightful rump, 'and tuck your hair under that cap on the seat.' He indicated a typical German working man's cap with its shiny peak.

She did as he ordered. He cranked the engine hastily. It sprang into noisy, shaky life almost instantly. He got into the van and put on a working man's cap himself. They started to move out of the parking lot.

'*Halt!*' the cry rang out.

In the headlights they could see the portly figure of the policeman who had looked at her earlier. He stood there arms out-stretched, face calm and untroubled, like that of a man who had always had his orders obeyed at once.

But the fat *schupo* had not reckoned with the tough Canadian at the wheel. 'Stupid bastard!' he growled and hit the horn hard in warning.

Still the policeman didn't move, confident that they would stop.

'All right, it's your funeral,' McIntyre grunted. He pressed his foot down on the accelerator of the little three-wheeler. At the very last minute the fat policeman attempted to jump out of the path of the flying van. Too late. The van struck him with such an impact that McIntyre feared they might stall for a moment. But the stout engine kept turning as the wheels ploughed over the *schupo,* leaving him sprawled groaning in the road.

A minute later the van was careering dangerously round the corner, scattering black, pressed-coal bricks behind it as it disappeared into the night.

Chapter Six

The last 24 hours had passed in hectic activity at the remote East Yorkshire port of Withernsea, as the crew of the *Swordfish* prepared for their mission. Supplies from nearby Hull had come in from the Royal Navy establishment there – extra fuel for the *Swordfish's* Thorneycroft engines, ammunition and brand-new Lewis guns ('C' had ordered that this time they should be prepared for any emergency), drift-mines for use in the river line, if necessary, and finally a guarded shipment of 1,000 sovereigns which might be needed to bribe the locals. For all the crew, even simple-minded Billy Bennett, knew that, unlike true Englishmen, foreigners liked to have their palms 'greased'. All foreigners were like that.

For that somewhat plump ex-sailor Billy Bennett, the rations they were taking aboard were the most important part of their stores for the mission. As he exclaimed to his old shipmate, red-headed Ginger Kerrigan, 'Plenty of bully and mashers and lashings of gravy.' He licked his lips, as if in anticipation, 'that's the stuff to give the troops,' to which Ginger had replied, looking at his round, honest face scornfully, 'Don't yer ever think of anything higher, old blubber-guts?'

'Like what?'

'A bit of the old grumble and grunt fer instance?'

CPO Ferguson, the ancient Scot who ran the *Swordfish,* had looked at Ginger Kerrigan severely and said, 'There'll be none of yon mucky blether while I'm in charge of you two. Get on with ye jobs.'

They did.

Now the *Swordfish* nosed her way slowly out into the North Sea, with Common Smith VC on the bridge, grateful for the damp, wet, grey sea fret. For the Special Branch detectives, who had been guarding their berth since they had arrived back in Withernsea, had informed him that they had 'reason to believe' that the *Swordfish* was being watched. From that, Smith had concluded that the sinister Lieutenant Commander von Horn, their old enemy, had his agents everywhere.

On the dripping deck, Dickie Bird had

assembled both watches under the craggy gaze of Chief Petty Officer Ferguson and was briefing them on their mission.

'All right, chaps,' he commenced as the seagulls dived through the mist, trying to pick up the slops which the cook had just thrown over, crying sadly like abandoned infants, 'Let me tell you what you're in for this time round.'

In the front rank, Ginger Kerrigan closed his eyes and pressed his hands together as if in solemn prayer, intoning, 'Thank you, Good Lord, for what we're about to receive.'

Some of the men laughed weakly. They all knew from long experience just how dangerous these secret missions for 'C' could be.

Ferguson snapped. 'None o' yon taking the Lord's name in vain, Kerrigan! And watch it, I've got my eye on ye.'

Bird smiled. Although he had been a civilian – officially – since 1918, the old Scot, who the crew maintained had sailed on HMS *Victory* with Nelson at the Battle of Trafalgar, was still very much the old-school petty officer.

'All right, you know we're off on a show. But not so far afield this time – Europe,' Bird said.

'Bluidy foreigners,' Ferguson growled, 'they're all the bluidy same, yon lot. Eating bits o' snails and yon worm-like stuff – spaghetti, or whatever the Dagoes call it.' He pulled a sour face.

'Now, now, Chiefie,' Dickie humoured him. 'Where's your spirit of Christian kindness?'

'The only spirit the Chiefie knows,' Ginger Kerrigan said cheekily, 'comes out of a whisky bottle. Look at the end of his nose!'

Ferguson glowered at him but said nothing.

Quickly, Bird carried out the briefing, telling them the river line they would patrol and that the Germans were planning to carry out some sort of major action against the withdrawing British Army before it reached the river line which marked Germany's frontier. He concluded with, 'I can't think at this stage of the game that it's going to be too dangerous except for the bit we'll have to travel down the Rhine in Germany.'

'Famous last words,' Sparks, the radio operator, groaned.

'We've done it before in Twenty-Three, as most of you remember,' Dickie continued, looking at their honest bronzed faces, telling himself that these men were risking their lives for a pittance, at the most £2 and keep a week. They complained naturally as sailors have always done ever since there had been a Royal Navy. But when the chips were down, they were prepared to fight for the honour of England and their shipmates to the bitter end, even if it meant death. 'So,' he continued, 'we've got to keep our eyes skinned all the time we're on the Rhine.'

'Like tinned tomatoes, sir,' Ginger said, ignoring CPO Ferguson's glare.

'Exactly, old chap.' Dickie Bird looked at Ferguson. 'A bit early, Chiefie, but I think it's time we spliced the mainbrace.'

Ferguson's craggy, lined face broke into a wintry smile. 'Ay, weel, sir, yon's a no bad idea.' He licked his wrinkled old lips in anticipation of the fierce rum soon to come.

Dickie Bird strode back to the bridge. 'The boys are in good heart, Smithie,' he commented, as down below Ferguson started to dish out the mugs of rum from the traditional little brass-bound keg.

'They always are,' Smith answered, peering through the white gloom. 'They're a good crowd. They don't come better.' He changed the subject. 'We'll make landfall after dawn tomorrow. The Dutch authorities have been bribed according to 'C', so we won't have any trouble with their Water Police of the *Rijkswacht*.'

He shrugged as the *Swordfish* plodded on through the sluggish, deep-green sea. 'But naturally there'll be informers among them who'll let the Huns know that we're on our way. The Hollanders played both sides of the fence in the last show, as you well know.'

Dickie Bird nodded a little gloomily, wondering how Smith was going to tackle the problem of getting from the Dutch-German frontier to Koblenz and the Moselle without serious trouble. Once in Koblenz they would be in the French Zone of Occupation and they'd be safe.

Common Smith seemed able to read his old friend's mind for he said, 'I suspect you're wondering how we're going to do it, especially now this von Horn Johnny knows we're onto them.'

Bird nodded.

Down below Billy Bennett, as greedy as ever, had swallowed his half-mug of dark brown in one swallow and was singing somewhat drunkenly, *'And the mate at the wheel was having a bloody good feel at the girl I left behind me... Where was the engine driver when the boiler bust? They found his bollocks...'*

'A barge,' Common Smith announced somewhat mysteriously.

'A barge,' Dickie Bird echoed. 'Oh my sainted aunt, what's that mean, old bean?'

' "C" has hired or bought, I don't know which, a Dutch barge at Dordrecht where we'll make landfall tomorrow. The Dutch authorities on the take from the Huns will see us enter and report accordingly, but thereafter we shall disappear.'

Dickie Bird pushed back his cap and scratched his head. 'You've lost me, old chap.'

'It's one of those large Dutch barges which work the Rhine trade from the sea to Strasbourg. Great big things. Well, we're going to be in the bowels of it as it sails up the German Rhine to Koblenz, where we shall leave.'

Dickie Bird's eyes lit up. 'What damned clever thinking on old "C's part. Didn't think he had it in him, the cunning old devil.'

Smith returned his smile in the same instant that CPO Ferguson came into the bridgehouse, eyes sparkling and nose looking redder than ever. 'Gentlemen,' he announced as if he were still back in the

Royal Navy 'Sparks had just had a signal from Scarborough.'

Smith's smile vanished at once. The hill above the Yorkshire seaside town on which the ruined medieval castle sat, was the royal Navy's signal station for this part of the coast. 'Yes?' he said urgently.

'Sparks says that they've spotted at least two, perhaps three, Jerry fishing smacks in the area, which is strange, ye ken, gentlemen, cos the Jerries ain't popular in these parts after their battleships bombarded Scarborough in December 1914.'

Smith nodded. He knew what the old CPO meant. Back at the beginning of the war the German High Fleet had slipped through Beatty's British Grand Fleet and had shelled Scarborough, Whitby and Hartlepool killing and wounding nearly 500 innocent men, women and children. The locals still bore a grudge against the Germans, particularly German fishermen in the area and they ran the risk of having their nets cut by the local fisherfolk.

'What else did they signal, Sparks?' he asked urgently.

'Not much gentlemen, except the Jerries don't appear to be doing much fishing. They've trawled their nets, but they're not doing it in the usual fashion.'

'How do you mean, Chiefie?' Dickie Bird asked.

'Well, you know they do it in a systematic fashion, moving about together very slowly to drive the fish into the nets. These Jerry trawlers seem to be spread all over the place and they're moving very fast for trawlers.'

Dickie looked significantly at Common Smith. 'They're looking for us, aren't they, Smithie.'

'Looks like it,' Smith answered easily, though his mind was racing hectically as he wondered what the *Swordfish's* next move should be. He stared out at the white mist. 'Well, we've got the sea fret on our side.' He made his decision. 'All the same we ought to be prepared for the worst.'

'How do you mean?'

'Alert the duty watch. If they spot one of those Jerry trawlers they're to sink it.'

Dickie Bird looked at his hold shipmate aghast. 'I say!' he exclaimed, 'that's a bit drastic, Smithie, isn't it? After all, we're not at war with the Hun, are we?'

Smith looked at him hard. 'Yes, we are. I think we've been at war, shooting and other-wise, since 1900. For all I know we'll be at war long after I'm dead. Perhaps right to the end of the century.' He sucked his front teeth thoughtfully and added, 'But for the time being let's worry about 1929. Stand the duty watch to, Dickie.' He turned to CPO Ferguson. 'Chiefie, tell Sparks I want radio silence till further notice. I don't want to give our position away unnecessarily.'

'Ay aye, sir,' Ferguson snapped dutifully, in Navy fashion, and went. A moment later Dickie Bird followed him to alert the crew, leaving Smith on the bridge alone with his thoughts.

They weren't particularly cheerful. This mission, he told himself, was going to be particularly dicey. The Huns knew that they were coming. Not only that, they also knew that the men of the *Swordfish* already were aware of what the German plan was, or at least some of it. In fact the enemy had most of the good cards in his hand.

Smith stared at the white pea-souper and told himself that this time he would have to play it bit by bit. There could be no long-term strategy. For now he would have to concentrate on getting the *Swordfish* across safely and link up with 'C's hired Dutch barge. So the *Swordfish* ploughed on into the grey-green waste of the North Sea, heading for her date with destiny.

Chapter Seven

'*Out*' McIntyre hissed in the pre-dawn stillness, with the sky flushed an ugly white to the east. He braked the three-wheeled van outside the coal merchants from which he had stolen it 48 hours before.

The girl needed no urging, knowing instinctively this was now the most dangerous part of their flight to Cologne. She slipped out of the van and stared at the white mist that covered the Rhine, shrouding the great span of the Hindenburg Bridge to her right.

He followed her a moment later, whispering, 'We're not going to swim for it, lassie. So don't worry. I've got it all planned – I hope!'

Instinctively she pressed his big, hard paw and said, 'I know you have, Major.'

'None o' that sissy stuff,' he growled, but he did so without resentment. He rather liked the affectionate gesture.

Together, almost noiselessly, they crossed the towpath that ran parallel to the Rhine.

All the same they were grateful for the mist, for the sounds coming from the Hohenzollern Bridge to their right indicated that the sentries up there were fully alert despite the lateness of the hour.

He halted and she clung to him, as if she couldn't bear not to feel his physical presence. 'I've got a little rowing boat down there among the bushes somewhere. The current is flowing about three knots from right to left. So we get in and do nothing until we've drifted to mid-stream then I start rowing–' He broke off suddenly.

'What is it?' she whispered anxiously.

'Be quiet!' he rasped. 'There's somebody coming.'

Now she, too, could hear the steady tread of heavy boots on the gravel of the towpath. The noise was paced and unhurried like that of someone going out for a leisurely stroll at this time of the day.

McIntyre knew it, too. He pushed to the side of the path and crouched low in front of her with his finger held to his lips in warning.

The footsteps came closer. Now the two fugitives could see the dim outline of a man set against the background of the white mist – and the figure carried a bayoneted rifle over his shoulder.

'Sentry,' McIntyre warned. 'Trouble. Not a sound, please.' He tensed, ready to go into action, knowing that he would have to quieten the man before he could sound the alarm. They'd have machine-guns on the German side of the great river and they wouldn't stand a chance against them while floating at three knots an hour. It was now or never. He drew a deep breath.

The sentry was almost parallel with them. For a moment McIntyre considered just letting the unsuspecting soldier walk past them. But then he told himself that as soon as they got into the boat he would hear them, and that would be that. The man had to be nobbled.

She touched his arm anxiously. He raised his right thumb as a sign that everything was all right. Next moment he had stolen from their cover and was creeping up behind the sentry. Then the man heard him. He turned and at the same time started hurriedly to unsling his rifle. McIntyre didn't give him a chance. He crooked his big arm around the man's throat and choked any cry he might have made. He grunted with the effort. In vain the sentry fought and writhed to free himself from that lethal hold. He gasped for breath, his mouth wide and gaping. She watched horrified. She had never seen anyone attempt to kill another person before – and this was exactly what McIntyre was trying to do.

The sentry's spine arched. He made one last desperate effort to break that terrible hold, as the rifle tumbled out of his almost nerveless fingers, but McIntyre was not to be denied. He exerted the last ounce of his strength, the sweat standing out on his forehead.

Suddenly, startlingly, the sentry's body went limp. It was all over. Carefully, very carefully, a panting, red-faced McIntyre relaxed his killing hold a little. No sound came from the sentry, whose tongue was hanging out of the side of his gaping mouth like a piece of red leather. He was dead. McIntyre lowered him to the ground and, as an afterthought, gave him a kick so that he tumbled into the drainage ditch at the side of the towpath and out of sight.

For what seemed an eternity McIntyre stood there, swaying slightly, as if he might be a little drunk, and gasping for breath. Then, in a voice that she could hardly recognize, he said hoarsely 'Come on, we'd better be off.'

Hastily they clambered down the muddy bank to the bushes where he had hidden the rowing boat two days before. It was still there. Hurriedly he held her cold hand as she stepped into it and undid the rope which tethered it to the bank, giving it a little shove with one oar. The current of the great river immediately seized the boat, which started to drift at a fair speed. Anxiously McIntyre glanced in the direction of the bridge and the positions of the German guards on the eastern side. Everything seemed calm. Apparently no one had heard the slight noise he had made.

Now they were heading for mid-stream and things seemed to be going well. Knowing how far sound carried over water, he whispered, 'I'll start rowing in about five minutes. Then with a bit of luck it'll take another five or ten minutes to reach the British side. We'll be safe then,' he added to comfort her, for he could sense just how frightened she was.

'Thank you, Major. You have been very kind to me.' She stopped short. 'What's that?' she hissed urgently.

He had heard the noise too: the steady chug-chug of a small boat's engine. It couldn't be that of a barge. These craft wouldn't ply their trade on the Rhine at night and under these foggy conditions. It had to be something else. For a few seconds he pretended to himself it was some local fisherman out looking for eels, which were a delicacy of this region when smoked. But even as he attempted to fool himself, he knew, with a sinking feeling, that eel-fishermen didn't have the money to buy boats equipped with petrol engines.

'Shit!' he cursed to himself angrily in the same instant that a light flashed on farther up the river, muted by the white fog, but there all right. He knew instinctively that it was a police boat belonging to the German *Wasserpolizei.*

She looked at him fearfully. 'What now?' she quavered.

He didn't answer. He could not because he didn't know himself what to do. As a last resort he pulled out the big Colt and hurriedly fitted the silencer to it.

The little launch chugged-chugged steadily towards them, its searchlight systematically sweeping from left to right, trying to penetrate the fog. Soon the beam would fall on the little boat and even the stupidest flatfoot, he told himself, would realize that there was something strange and suspicious about a rowing boat floating in the Rhine in the middle of the night.

He made his decision. 'Keep down!' he commanded urgently and raised the pistol. He balanced himself the best he could in the slightly swaying rowing boat and rested the pistol on his left forearm for more accuracy. He knew he'd only get one bite of the cherry. He had to knock out that searchlight with his first shot, there would not be the chance for a second. All the launches of the German *Wasserpolizei* were equipped with light machine-guns mounted just behind the bridge and the cops, veterans of the Great War, would not hesitate to use that gun. They'd shoot the rowing boat to matchwood.

He steadied himself and controlled his breathing. He took first pressure, all tension vanished. 'All right, try this on for size,' he rasped to himself and pulled the trigger.

Plop. The muzzle of the big, heavy Colt jerked upwards. There was a tinkle of broken glass, an angry curse and the light went out, leaving the two of them blinking in the sudden darkness. McIntyre seized the oars, which he had already wrapped with old rags at the level of the rowlocks to muffle the sound and began to pull away swiftly before the Germans reacted.

Brrr! Angry scarlet flame stabbed the darkness. Tracer zipped lethally across the Rhine. McIntyre, straining at the oars, could hear the slugs slap harmlessly into the water. But he knew their luck wouldn't hold out for ever. The Germans would be expert enough to fan the surface of the Rhine with their machine-gun. It wouldn't be long before they would be in danger.

The girl seemed to sense that, too. She gave a little shriek of fear and gasped, 'Are we going to make it?'

'Of course,' he muttered with more confidence in his voice than he actually felt. 'The Huns have got to get up a damned sight earlier than this to catch Mrs Bridie McIntyre's handsome son.' He shut up and concentrated on the rowing.

Again another savage burst of machine-gun fire sliced the air just above the surface of the Rhine. The gunner was getting closer to them, McIntyre knew that. What could he do? He didn't know whether the girl could swim or not. Besides if they went over the side the current would slow them down and they would be even more of an easy target.

He stopped rowing and took a chance. Raising his pistol he tried to guess where the boat was. If he was lucky he'd knock out the machine-gun.

But Fate took a hand in the deadly game. In the instant that he decided he'd fight it out, a loud cockney voice said, 'Hey, what the bloody hell is going on?'

A light flicked on, and another. In the one beam a thick-set figure in khaki uniform, his bayonet raised threateningly, was outlined, looking for all the world like 'Old Bill' of the wartime cartoons of Captain Bainsfather.

'Don't yer bleedin' know that this is 'inglish' territory? Now bugger off yer Jerry sods.'

The stout figure with the old-fashioned walrus moustache thrust forward his bayonet as if he were back in the war and about to plunge it into some Hun who refused to surrender.

McIntyre waited tensely but not for long. Suddenly the engine of the motor launch revved up and it was turning about, speeding back to its berth. Old Bill had done the trick.

Five minutes later the two of them were drinking steaming-hot 'sarnt-major's char' in which a spoon would stand up, with the Old Bill saying stoutly, 'We saw off old Kaiser Bill in the last show, sir. It'd take more of them modern Jerries to frighten old Jem 'awkins.'

For once, McIntyre's hard face relaxed, as next to him in the guard post the other sentry telephoned HQ. He felt relaxed and grateful. These old Tommies, the best kind who had served in the trenches right from 1914, had saved their bacon at the very last moment when he had felt they were about done for. Now he had completed the mission assigned to him and with a bit of luck Fraulein Lena could be able to tell them more about what was going on in the German camp.

He looked over the rim of the chipped enamel mug at the girl. She was a prostitute, he knew, and the part-time mistress of the old general from the 'Cherrypickers', but what appealed to him was her fragile kind of beauty, with none of that brassy hardness of the professional whore. All his life he had taken women when he had needed them, mostly paying for their services. In his line of business, ever since he had come from Canada in 1914 as a private in 'Hell's Last Issue', otherwise the Canadian Highland Light Infantry, he had had no time for romance, that 'sissy shit', as he had always considered it. Life had been too short and too brutal for entanglements of that kind. Now, sitting in the little wooden hut that smelled of human sweat, coarse tobacco and creosote, he felt an emotion for the German woman that was completely novel for him.

Instinctively, hardly knowing what he was doing, he reached out his big paw and pressed her skinny little hand gently. 'Everything's going to be all right,' he said. 'You can rely on me.'

She looked across at him, her pale blue eyes suddenly brimming with tears for reasons known only to her. 'I know I can, Major,' she said fervently, in the same instant that the elderly lance-corporal at the phone clicked to attention and barked, 'Headquarters, sir!'

McIntyre put down his mug and strode over to the green-painted field telephone. For a few minutes he listened attentively to the authoritative upper-class voice at the other end, occasionally snapping, 'Understood, sir... Clear... Will do, sir.' Then he put the phone down, reached in his jacket and pulled out his battered leather wallet and took a £5 note out. He handed it to the old soldier with the walrus moustache. 'Here you are. Thanks, boys, for everything.'

'Old Bill' looked at it incredulously. 'Cor',

ferk a duck,' he exclaimed, 'a big white one, Nobby! Keep us in wallop for a month of Sundays. Thank *you* very much, sir!'

McIntyre forced a smile as he steered the girl out of the little guardhouse into the cold dawn. 'Things are moving,' he snapped once he knew that the two Tommies couldn't hear them any more. 'They need us at HQ. And Fraulein Lena–' he added hesitantly.

'Yes, Major?'

McIntyre flushed for the first time in his life since he had left his elementary school in the Gorbals.

She repeated her query.

'Do ... do you think ... I can see you again?'

Chapter Eight

'Did I ever tell yer about the tart I had in Calais during the war who had two sets o' tits, Billy?' Ginger Kerrigan asked lazily as he watched the first rays of the September sun begin to sweep away the mist to the east.

'Yer,' his tubby companion said, chewing

his way through one of his favourite bully beef sandwiches, while he stared to port on the lookout for the German trawlers they had been warned about the night before. 'But yer gonna tell me agen, I know.'

Ginger didn't seem to hear. He said, 'Well, I'd got me hand up her jumper.'

Billy Bennett scoffed the rest of his sandwich, belched rather politely for him – and yawned deliberately.

'Well, as I was saying, I'd got my hands up there and what d'yer know?'

'Yer found her first set o' tits and then yer found the other tits, and that put yer right off cos yer diamond cutter vanished straight off,' Billy Bennett mimicked his old ship-mate savagely.

Ginger stared at him hard. 'Yer don't look a bad bloke, Billy Bennett, but I swear yer a bad bugger really–' He broke off suddenly. 'To starboard,' he rasped urgently.

Billy swung up his binoculars, the good-natured banter forgotten. A red-sailed fishing smack swept silently into the circles of calibrated glass. 'Jerry!' he exclaimed almost at once. 'The cheese-eaters and us has different sets of sails.'

'My thinking as well, Billy,' Ginger said urgently. He cupped his hands to his mouth.

'Attention, bridge!' He yelled against the stiff wind blowing in from the dark smudge of land on the horizon, which was Holland.

'What is it?' Dickie Bird leaned out of the bridgehouse and called back. 'Where's the deuced fire?'

'Jerry fishing smack to starboard, sir,' Ginger answered promptly. 'Could be trouble.'

Dickie Bird immediately flung up his own binoculars and stared through them at the smack with the red sail. 'Oh my sainted aunt!' he groaned. 'You're right.' He let his binoculars fall to his chest and strode over to the voice-tube. He uncorked and whistled down it to attract Smith's attention in the cramped wardroom below. 'Smithie,' he snapped.

'Yes,' Common Smith answered a little wearily. He had been on duty all night since the trawler alert and had just manage to catch an hour's sleep on the battered horse-hair sofa in the wardroom.

'Huns.'

'The trawlers?'

'Yes, one of them at least.' Smith was wide awake immediately. He replied, 'Coming up topside immediately.'

Together the two comrades stared as the

red-sailed trawler came closer, gliding across the still dawn sea in sinister silence, heading on what appeared to be a collision course for the *Swordfish*. Now they could see the tiny black figures moving about her deck, but they didn't appear in any hurry. All the same they were not attempting to keep up their guise as fishermen. No nets were down and holds that would hold fish caught were firmly covered.

'What do you think?' Bird asked after a while surveying the German craft.

'I don't quite know, to be frank,' Common Smith answered in some bewilderment. 'It's obvious they know where we are and who we are. They're coming straight at us after all. But I can't see any sign of guns or other offensive weapons.'

He stopped short suddenly. 'Christ Almighty!' he exclaimed in sudden alarm.

'What is it?'

'Look. The craft's port bow.'

Hurriedly Dickie Bird focused his glasses. Some kind of trapdoor was being slid back to the port of the fishing smack just above the waterline and he thought he caught a glimpse of something metallic glimmering in the first rays of the dawn sun. 'What is it, Smithie?'

'Don't you know?'

Dickie Bird shook his head.

'A torpedo hatch ... some kind of make shift one at least.'

'Oh, my sainted aunt!' Dickie began in the same moment that there was a hard noise like metal striking metal followed an instant later by the hiss of compressed air. A flurry of bubbles broke the surface at the barge's bows and for one fleeting moment they caught a glimpse of an urgent white V of water streaking towards them.

'*Torpedo!*' Bird yelled.

At the wheel, CPO Ferguson reacted with surprising speed and agility for a man of his age. He spun the wheel to starboard. *Swordfish* heeled dramatically and for a moment it looked as if its wireless mast would touch the water. At the bow Billy Bennett was thrown against a stanchion with a cry of 'Hell's bells, what the frig's going on?'

A second later he saw what 'the frig was going on' as the torpedo flashed by the *Swordfish* with only yards to spare. 'Well, I'm a dipstick!' he yelled, 'They've fired a tin fish at us!'

They certainly had and now on the starboard bow another trapdoor was sliding back to reveal yet another ton of high explosive cased in steel.

'Gawd Almighty!' Dickie Bird said, 'It's like the war, trying to out-guess the Hun. Which way will he fire?'

'Well, we'd better do it, *and soon*,' Common Smith answered swiftly. 'Because they're going to attempt to stick another one up us in half a mo! Look!'

The torpedo was already beginning to run. They could see the water churning wild, white and angry as the weapon's motor was activated.

'What now, brown cow?' Dickie Bird asked urgently.

'Full steam ahead and damn the torpedoes, as someone once said,' Smith yelled, suddenly carried away by the wild, unreasoning illogic of battle. 'Chiefie,' he yelled, 'Up Guards and at 'em!'

The wizened old chief petty officer needed no urging. He applied the throttles and the *Swordfish* surged forward. In a flash her upper deck tilted and a great white bone erupted at her bows. In an instant she was surging forward at 40 knots, her deck quivering under their feet. She shot forward, closing with the red-sailed fishing smack by the second. On the deck of the German craft, the crew had pulled the

89

tarpaulin off a concealed machine-gun. Tracer, red and deadly, sped towards the British vessel. At the wheel CPO Ferguson spun the motor launch from side to side as the tracer whizzed by them, missing the *Swordfish* by what appeared to be inches.

Common Smith made his decision. 'Chiefie!' he yelled, 'I'll take over the wheel. Get Ginger and Billy Bennett to break out the Lewis guns. I'm going after the sods. It's the only way.'

'Ay ay, sir.' Hurriedly Ferguson left the wheelhouse and started shouting out orders to the deck watch.

'Heaven help a sailor on a night like this,' Dickie Bird intoned, as his old shipmate opened the throttle even more so that the *Swordfish* shuddered violently as she hit every wave; it was like running into a series of walls.

On the German craft the two machine-gunners were systematically hosing the sea to the *Swordfish's* front. It was like a wall of white tracer. Here and there bits of the *Swordfish's* rigging came tumbling down in disarray. But still, his face set and hard, Common Smith steered the motor launch directly at the German fishing smack. It loomed larger and larger by the instant.

Crouching next to his skipper, Dickie Bird could see every detail of her distinctly as down below, Ginger and Billy Bennett worked frantically to set up the ugly-looking Lewis machine-gun, while CPO Ferguson cursed them and urged them to ever greater speed.

'Ready!' Billy Bennett shouted as he slapped the round pan of ammunition on the top of the heavy weapon. Ginger didn't waste any time, he slammed the heavy butt of the machine-gun into his shoulder and squinted along the thick, ugly barrel. He knew exactly what to do, without orders. He would take out the gunner at the bow and at the same time hose the two ports from which the torpedoes had been fired just in case the Germans attempted to fire more.

Bracing himself against the hectic heaving and trembling of the *Swordfish* going all out now at 40 knots and peering through the twin curves of wild white water thrown up at her bow, he pressed the trigger. The Lewis gun chattered into frantic life. Suddenly the clean dawn air was full of the acrid stink of burned cordite. Tracer zipped lethally towards the fishing smack and wood splinters flew from the deck. There the first German machine-gunner threw up his arms melodramatically and reeled backwards, his face torn to bloody shreds by that terrible burst. Next moment he fell to the blood-stained deck, dead before he hit it.

In the very last moment Common Smith spun the wheel round. There seemed only inches between the two craft. Hastily the second German machine-gunner fired a rapid burst ripping the length of the *Swordfish*. The wireless mast came tumbling down with a series of angry blue sparks and the wireless operator came rushing out of his shack, crying. 'You bloody 'Uns! Now look what yer've frigging well done. I can't send...!'

Common Smith spun the wheel round again. He was going in for another attack, carried away by the unreasoning blood lust of battle. Down below Ginger slapped on another pan of ammunition and commenced firing once more. On the fishing smack panicking sailors ran back and forth. But Ginger could see another torpedo beginning to protrude from the port hatch. 'Bastards!' he cursed to himself. 'Think you've got our goose cooked. Well, you've got another frigging think coming.' Ignoring the second machine-gunner, he concentrated on the hatch, peppering the area all around it with slugs. The timbers splintered and flew apart like matchwood. Still the unseen torpedo men pushed their tin fish forward, ready to activate it at any moment and this time an angry, frantic Ginger knew they wouldn't miss at that range.

Still Common Smith pressed home his attack as he had done in that celebrated assault on Petrograd harbour and the Russian Red Fleet which had won him what the press had called back in 1918 'the secret VC'.*

Suddenly Ginger Kerrigan struck lucky. He ripped off a burst at the emerging torpedo. Fortune was on his side as somehow or other his burst struck the torpedo's detonator as it began to run. It was just about to drop into the water and bring *Swordfish's* long career to a final end when the ton of high explosive exploded. One moment the fishing smack was there, the next it had disappeared in a burst of angry flame and smoke. Wood and pieces of human bodies rained down on the *Swordfish* as the deck watch gazed in awe at the terrible spectacle of another ship being done to violent death.

*See Charles Whiting, *The Baltic Run*

Then Smith was reducing the *Swordfish's* speed, trying to avoid the shattered debris everywhere littering the heaving, churning sea. Billy Bennett stared at the severed, tattooed arm which had abruptly landed at his feet on the deck and was violently sick where he stood.

Chapter Nine

Von Horn listened attentively as the assistant naval attaché reported from The Hague, nodding at intervals as he absorbed the details of the failed attack by the camouflaged fishing smack. Finally he said, 'They are cunning these English. It has always been my principle never to trust an Englishman, especially when he purports to be a gentleman. They are the worst kind. However,' he ended, 'keep an eye on them. We shall see off the *gentlemen*,' he emphasized the word bitterly, 'of the *Swordfish* before many days are over. *Ende.*' The line went dead and he put down his own phone.

For a while he sat in the big, bare office reflecting on what he had just learned.

Outside, the recruits were going through their paces under the command of some hoarse-voiced petty officer. 'Enemy to the right!' he was bellowing, 'Open fire!' And the recruits banged their naked bayonets against their thighs to simulate guns firing.

Von Horn frowned. Those traitors in Berlin wouldn't spend a penny on the Navy, so the recruits were reduced to playing games like silly schoolboys. But once 'Wolf' took over power things would change. Germany would recommence its holy mission of becoming master of Europe. Then there would be plenty of money for the Navy. Things would change, very definitely.

He forgot the recruits and their silly games and concentrated on the task at hand. Once the damned *Swordfish* was in German waters, it and its crew would be taken care of once and for all. He would have no further trouble with Lieutenant Smith. He dismissed the *Swordfish*, as if that particular problem was already solved.

Von Horn picked up the phone. 'Send in the signals officer,' he commanded the operator.

A few minutes later the young lieutenant in charge of signals at intelligence head-quarters appeared and again von Horn rapped out his orders in that harsh, arrogant manner of his. 'Signal our consulate in New York that we are ready now for the Hell's Angels. They must be prepared to sail at once. Germany's destiny is at stake.'

The handsome young signals officer looked up from his signals at the last words and looked searchingly at his superior. But the latter gave no clue as to why he had selected such serious words. So he continued taking down the rest of the signal to New York before venturing a cautious, 'But who are these, er, Hell's Angels, *Herr Kapitanleutnant?*'

Von Horn gave the young signals officer one of his crooked, cynical grins. ''Fraid I can't tell you that at this moment, Goetz. But, never fear, you'll be hearing of them soon – the whole world will.' With a wave of his hand he dismissed the other officer and sat back in his chair, well pleased with himself. The stage was set, the actors were almost in place, the drama could commence...

PART TWO

Chapter One

'For God's sake,' Horst von Hechlingen said with a smile, 'don't forget to put on the frilly knickers. We don't want the hicks to see that great hairy thing dangling down,' As usual the Hell's Angels mixed in the American slang words when they spoke their own language together.

'Holy strawsack,' Dietz exclaimed, 'I almost forgot.' He pulled up the short, flapper's frock which he wore for his part of the show and reaching for the knickers he pulled them up his brawny, muscular thighs.

Outside, the local high school band, hired at $5 for the afternoon, were giving a very poor rendering of a Sousa march, while the popcorn and hot dog vendors called their wares among the crowd of hicks who had come from all over the county to watch, as their posters proclaimed, 'The most daring and audacious fliers on this side of the Atlantic – THE HELL'S ANGELS'.

As soon as Dietz had pulled on the knickers, the flask of whisky went the rounds, as was their customary habit just before take-off. Most of them had been together since the days of the Red Baron. Throughout the war they had drunk and flown, knowing that their lives might be cut off at any moment. It had been no different after the fighting had ceased when they had refused to surrender to the victorious allies and had used the stolen squadron funds to smuggle themselves into Canada and from there, in due course, to the United States. There they had begun their barnstorming career in wartime Sopwith Camels bought from US Army surplus, travelling back and forth across the country taking 'hicks', as they had learned to call them, for $5 flights, staging mock air battles and giving displays of low-level flying which had had the crowds gasping.

Occasionally they had accidents and would bury the body of their dead comrade to the tune of an old recording of the German Army song 'Ich hatte einen Kameraden' plus a lot of alcohol. For in the end, as blasé and fatalistic as they were in this strange, self-imposed exile, they knew they would all die violently.

'Well,' Dietz said, adjusting the skimpy dress and putting on the white helmet and goggles which he would wear for his performance, 'here's to the next man to die. Suppose we ought to get on with it.'

They nodded, tossed off the rest of their bourbon and filed outside into the blinding sunlight, scar-faced men in their early thirties who risked death every day for a handful of dollars, a drink or two and some raddled whore in a cheap bar who could be bought for 50 cents.

Immediately the high school band broke into the 'March of the Gladiators' and the pilots started to strut instinctively as they had done in the proud old days when they had been officers and gentlemen in the old Imperial German Army, parading in front of some royal prince or other just behind the front in France.

Ex-*Hauptmann* von Pritzwitz, with his sabre-scarred face and shaved bullet-head, was waiting for them, scowling through the monocle he affected. 'Where have you been, you lazy swine?' he cried to the microphone so that the crowd could hear. 'We cannot wait for you for ever. And you,' he glowered at Dietz, 'pull your skirt down, you wanton hussy.' He winked at the younger man. It was all part of the act. They were the good guys and he was the Prussian swine. The crowd didn't know that; they hooted and booed and some drunk yelled, 'I ought to have killed you off in the Argonne back in '18, you Heinie bastard!'

The pilots and stuntmen tried to keep a straight face as behind them the mechanics, also German, started up the 'stringbags', as they called the battered old wartime fighters, which in some cases were held together by twine and wire.

The Prussian *Hauptmann* slapped the riding crop he carried against a highly polished boot and yelled, 'Well, you now get to work, you bunch of drunken rogues. These people have paid plenty of money to see your miserable performance – fifty American cents. *Los, Maenner!*'

The best they could, as if they were back in the war scrambling for an enemy attack, they doubled across the rough field to their old planes, with Dietz worrying whether the elastic in the frilly white knickers would hold for the show. It had happened before that the elastic had snapped and he had fallen flat on his face with his naked rump in the air and the knickers around his ankles to the delight of the onlookers. For a while they had considered whether they should make it part of the act, but in the end they had decided against it for, as Dietz had said, 'You can't expect a former member of Richthofen's Flying Circus to show his crown jewels twice a day to a bunch of ignorant American yokels, can you!'

Dietz clambered onto the wing of the biplane and men in the crowd whistled and made lewd remarks as they looked up his skimpy frock. Dietz was used to it, but still it rankled a little that he had to go through this business just to stay alive when once he had been a celebrated hero, holder of the 'Blue Max' with a stable of wealthy, beautiful mistresses. He took hold of the strut from which he would commence his wing-walking once they were airborne. He nodded to Horst von Hechlingen, who was his pilot today, *'Alles klar, Horst?'*

'Okay, baby,' Horst, whose father had once been a field marshal in the Bavarian Army, replied in his American English. He cupped his hands around his mouth and shouted to the mechanic holding the rope which kept the chocks against the wheels, *'Los, Kinkel, wir starten.'*

The mechanic tugged the rope. The chocks fell away and Horst opened the throttle. The plane started to bump its way forward, Dietz holding on to the stanchion, the flapper frock billowing about his hips and displaying the frilly white knickers above his shaven thighs. 'Here we go again,' he said to himself, as the wind started to tug at him and tried to tear him from his precarious perch. 'Yet once more a death-defying act.' He grinned in spite of the tears the wind brought to his eyes.

But this day there was going to be no more 'death-defying acts'. Suddenly a long, gleaming Cadillac came bouncing across the field in the path of the advancing Camels, flashing its lights, with the uniformed chauffeur sounding his horn urgently.

'What in three devils' names is going on?' Horst, the pilot, cried angrily, adding, 'Is that guy nuts?'

At the makeshift control tower, ex-*Hauptmann* von Pritzwitz fired his signal pistol, indicating they should stop the show. Obediently, the first three pilots throttled back and came to a halt, Dietz trying to pull down his frock so that the chauffeur couldn't look up it as the Cadillac, slowing down, but still sounding its horn urgently, came parallel with them.

A pompous-looking man with a silver-topped cane sat bolt upright in the back, dressed in a morning suit complete with top hat. Resolutely, he refused to look at Dietz, as if he took him to be a real woman of some vulgarity, displaying her body like that.

Dietz laughed and then Horst was wheeling the plane about as the puzzled crowd booed and gave them the 'Bronx cheer', heading back to where the *Hauptmann* and the stranger in the Cadillac waited for them.

The *Hauptmann* beamed as Dietz got off the wing and said, 'Young feller, you'll never need to wear frilly knickers again.'

The pompous-looking man in the top hat frowned. He barked in the arrogant accent of the German Prussian aristocracy, 'I knew your father, the General. I am sure, perfectly sure, that he would not have approved of his son wearing – er – frilly knickers. It's perverted!'

The others laughed carelessly, and Dietz said, 'I agree with you one hundred per cent. But that's the way the world is today for us poor Germans. You know what the Sammies say' – he meant the Americans – "another day, another dollar."'

'*Schon gut,*' *Hauptmann* von Pritzwitz cut in harshly in his Prussian manner, 'enough of this idle chatter. The mission has come

105

through. We're going back this very day. We shall sail from New York's Pier Twenty-Four this night.'

There was a ragged cheer from the assembled pilots and crew members. A couple of the ground crew shook hands with each other. On the benches the spectators and the high school band launched into a very ragged version of the 'Stars and Stripes for Ever'.

Dietz grinned and bending down said, 'Up the damned "Stars and Stripes".' He removed the knickers in question as he did so, revealing his naked bottom to the astonished, suddenly shocked crowd. They fell silent as he threw the knickers in the direction of the spectators. 'Goodbye, America!' he yelled defiantly and then in German, *'Es lebe Deutschland!'*

Perhaps the crowd didn't understand the expression 'Long live Germany', but they took the German words as some kind of insult and began to jeer and boo again.

The pompous man from the New York consulate looked worried. He barked, 'Enough of this foolish play acting. We must waste no further time. Now every hour is precious.

The *Hauptmann* clicked to attention. Just

as he might have done in the war, he raised his right hand stiffly to his white flying helmet and rasped. *'Jawohl, Herr Legationsrat. Melde gehorsamte. Geschwader 52 zur Stelle.'*

Slightly taken aback, the man from the consulate raised his top hat and stuttered *'Danke.* Your transport is on its way. You can see them.' He pointed to the long, white coach, followed by a succession of Dodge trucks which were now rolling onto the field, while the crowd watched them in a mixture of derision and astonishment, wondering exactly what was going on. Someone yelled, 'Give us our dough back, you Heinie bastards!'

'Tell them they will have their money refunded,' the man in the top hat said hastily. 'Now let us get you to your transport. The mechanics can start getting planes broken down ready for the trucks. Come along now please. You are needed in the Reich.' He gave them a fake, diplomatic smile. 'You are going home again, gentlemen!'

Suddenly the enormity of that statement hit them. Their hard, cynical looks, the product of four years of battle and ten years in exile, vanished. 'In God's name,' Dietz said in an awed voice, tears flooding his eyes abruptly, 'You're right ... we *are* going home!'

Humbled and in silence they walked over to the coach, while the high school band played away madly and the crowd, silent too now that they were going to get their money back, watched and wondered.

Five minutes later they were on their way, heading down the state highway towards New York and the freighter which would take them across the Atlantic. The Hell's Angels were going home at last to fight their last battle.

Chapter Two

'Dordrecht,' Smith announced as the *Swordfish* came to rest at the cobbled quayside and the anchor chain rattled down. 'We'll inform the harbour master that we're here for two days and pay the port dues for that period of time. But as soon as it's really dark, 'C's barge will come for us – and we're off.'

'Jolly good show!' Dickie Bird said, eyeing the buxom fisherwomen in their clogs, skirts tucked into knickers, as they gutted the tiny herrings, which the Dutch liked to eat raw, before tossing them into great barrels of brine.

Next to Dickie, CPO Ferguson pulled a sour face. 'Foreigners and their fodder. They dinna ken no decent food like fish an' taties or haggis and nips. No, they're always scoffing muck like that. Why, them yellow chinks eat rotten eggs that are a hundred years old!'

Smith smiled. The old Chiefie had spent all his life travelling the world, but he never had a good word to say for foreigners. Indeed, Smith often imagined that the grizzled old Scot had little time for anyone who hadn't been born north of the border!

Slowly, as the *Swordfish's* engines died away, the men of the deck watch relaxed from their duties, glancing up at the bridgehouse frequently. Smith knew why. They were wondering if the skipper was going to allow a couple of hours shore leave.

Ferguson looked stern. 'Ye ne gonna let that randy bunch ashore, are ye?' he snapped, knowing the significance of the looks. 'Yon place'll be full o' hoors and they'll only get their sens in muckle trouble. Ye ken what they're like, sir.'

Dickie Bird grinned and said, 'Have a heart, Chiefie. They've got to get some of the dirty water off their chests. We aren't running a monastery, you know.'

'Damned Papists,' Ferguson spat routinely. 'Yon Pope in Rome has got a lot to answer for, I'll be thinking.'

Smith flashed a look at his watch and made his decision. 'As soon as I've been to the harbour master's office to pay the port dues, stand half the duty watch down. They can have two hours on the town. See that someone armed goes with them and they're not to stray.'

'*Stray!*' Ferguson said contemptuously. 'Ye ken where that lot will be like a flash. In the nearest knocking shop.' He shook his head like a man being sorely tried but left the bridgehouse to carry out Smith's order dutifully enough.

'I hope the cheese-eaters have got something with chips,' Billy Bennett said eagerly, as the little crowd of sailors hurried down the quayside, heavy with the stink of oil and raw fish. 'I could just go a plate o'chips with bangers and perhaps half a dozen fried eggs. Luvverly grub, Ginger, eh!'

His companion looked up at the big portly sailor and sneered, 'Ain't yer got no romance in yer friggin' soul? All you think about is yer guts. There's other things in life than egg and friggin' chips.'

Billy Bennett looked at Ginger, pretending to be puzzled, 'What, fer instance?' he asked, as if he meant the question seriously.

'All right,' snapped Ferguson, who was acting as guard, with a revolver bulging from the pocket of his rough tweed jacket. 'Just march right smart to that knocking shop over yonder and let's get on with it, ye bunch o' filthy matelots, with yer brains between yer friggin' shanks.'

The harbour master was a big, fat, jolly man who smoked a curved pipe and smelled strongly of *genever*, the Dutch gin, but at the same time Smith noted that his dark eyes beneath the thick, bushy eyebrows were very shrewd and calculating. The harbour master also asked what Smith thought were too many questions for what should have been a simple transaction of paying for the berth.

In the end, Smith pleaded he had a lot of work to do and left but when he looked back once outside the door, he could see the fat harbour master peering at him from the window and this time he wasn't looking very jolly at all. Automatically Smith told himself that if anyone was working for von Horn in

Dordrecht it would be the Dutchman. They would have to take care when they made the night-time transfer to 'C's barge.

Ginger Kerrigan was not worried about such matters at that moment. The brothel was packed with fat, tall women, mostly sitting in their petticoats and drinking beer from litre-sized glasses which they kept on the floor between their spread legs – and Ginger noted immediately that all of them were without their knickers. As he remarked to Billy, 'Old shipmate, you're not buying a pig in a poke in this place. You can see exactly what they've got on offer.'

'Plenty,' Billy agreed, 'and I don't fancy it with chips. Ha, ha!'

Ginger scowled at him. 'This is serious, yer know,' he commented, 'We're not talking about yer bloody chips. We're talking grumble and grunt.'

Billy Bennett nodded. 'I suppose yer right, Ginger. Yer've got to have a bit o' romance in yer soul.'

'Too bloody true. Now come on, let's get at it!' He rushed forward to the nearest whore and said in what he imagined was a foreign accent, 'You speaka da English?'

Outside, just by the door in one of the stiff, upright chairs vacated by the whores at the prospect of trade, CPO Ferguson sighed and muttered to himself that 'with yon lot, some of them'll be getting thesens a nasty souvenir, I'll be bound.' Then he forgot the 'hoors' and the diseases they might well transmit to the crewmen from the *Swordfish* and stared moodily to his front, puffing at his old white clay pipe as he did so.

'Hello there, Engelsman,' the hearty voice broke into his reverie.

Ferguson opened his half-closed eyes. A fat, jolly man with a walrus moustache stood there, beaming down at him, hands clasped across his ample stomach, laden with watch chains and ornaments.

'Hello,' he answered, wondering what the foreigner wanted from him. Foreigners in his experience, always wanted something from an honest Scot or tried to sell you something, usually obscene.

'The boys, they have a good time, eh,' the fat Dutchman said, pointing upstairs with the stem of his pipe, from whence the rapid squeak of rusty bedsprings came.

Ferguson nodded in a non-committal sort of manner, wishing the foreigner would go away and allow him to doze in peace in the hazy September sunshine.

'You stay long in Dordrecht?' the Dutchman asked, as if it wasn't important, though an astute observer would have noted the keen look in his dark eyes.

'Two days,' Ferguson answered.

'Then where?'

Ferguson had had enough. 'None of ye business,' he snapped.

The Dutchman wasn't offended. 'Well,' he said, 'have a good time in old Holland. *Tot ziens.*' And with that he strolled away as if he had all the time in the world, leaving Ferguson to half-close his eyes, trying to cut out the sounds from the 'knocking shop' and doze.

Half an hour later, the fat harbour master was talking on the phone to von Horn in fluent German. He told the spymaster what he knew and after a while von Horn snapped, 'It's them all right. Keep an eye on them. It is to your advantage. We pay well.'

'*Jawohl,*' the Dutchman answered. He had worked for German Intelligence from neutral Holland all throughout the war; he knew the '*Moffen*', as the Dutch nicknamed the Germans, paid well. Now that things were beginning to look up for a defeated Germany he anticipated that they would be paying well again. He hung up.

By now it was beginning to grow dark. The second half of the crew had taken their pleasures in the brothel and had been allowed to drink a few glasses of Dutch beer. They had been fed. 'Bully beef fritters, that's the right kind of scoff for our kind,' Ferguson had commented with some kind of satisfaction, for him. 'None o' that foreign muck.'

Now they were businesslike again, ready for the link-up with the barge that would take them through the Rhineland.

Over in the town the house lights had gone out. There was no sound. Even the brothel was silent. It appeared that Holland went to bed early, something for which Smith was glad. His plan was to slip the *Swordfish's* anchor just at midnight when the big church clock would chime twelve. The sound of the chimes should cover any noise the anchor chain would make. Then he'd allow the *Swordfish* to drift downstream with the current to meet the barge. As he explained to Dickie Bird, who, like all the crew was now armed, 'There might well be someone watching us, indeed, I'd be surprised if there wasn't. But they might be taking a little snooze by this time. Anyway I hope we effectively disappear once the barge picks us up.'

'Famous last words,' Dickie Bird said in his usual flippant manner, though underneath there was a serious tone to his voice. He knew, like the rest of the *Swordfish's* crew, that the German spymaster von Horn would show them no mercy if they ever fell into his hands. They'd disappear for good, they had been a thorn in his flesh for too long.

Now the minutes started to pass by rapidly on the silent, darkened quayside. As the illuminated hands of the big clock came ever closer to twelve, the crew tensed. At the anchor chain the two ratings who would drag up the anchor prepared to move. In the bridgehouse Smith spun the wheel round ready to direct the *Swordfish* into the down-river current. The clock's hands touched midnight and in a heavy, sombre tone the chimes commenced ringing out.

Immediately the two ratings started to slip the anchor almost noiselessly dragging up the chain which had been well greased beforehand. Smith waited until the dripping anchor had cleared the water and Ferguson whistled softly to signal that it had cleared the surface and the *Swordfish* was free from any restraint. Smith waited another moment

116

or two. Already the clock had chimed eight and despite the coldness of the night he felt himself beginning to sweat with tension. At the railing the deck watch heaved and thrust their boathooks against the green-slimed covered stone wall. Slowly almost reluctantly, or so it seemed to a worried Smith, the *Swordfish* began to move.

Hastily Smith steered her into the current, which took hold of *Swordfish*. Her speed started to quicken, and Smith told himself they were doing it. He flashed a look at the land. Nothing stirred. Nobody was observing their silent departure. Tomorrow morning, he told himself triumphantly, the fat harbour master, if he really was working for the Germans, would have to report to von Horn that the *Swordfish* had vanished without trace.

At the bow, peering through his night glasses, Dickie Bird was not so sanguine. As the old church clock sounded the last chime of midnight, he spotted a faint white light blinking on and off. For a moment or two he told himself that it might be the defective headlights of some lone car. But then he realized there was a pattern to the flashing off and on. Someone was signalling in morse code. He could read the letters, but could make no sense of the signal, for it was in a language – perhaps Dutch – which he didn't understand. 'Blast and damn it!' he cursed to himself. 'They've bloody well spotted us after all!'

He let the night glasses fall to his chest and sprinted across the deck towards the bridgehouse. Hastily he clattered up to the bridge as the *Swordfish* continued to gain speed, leaving the sleeping Dutch port behind them.

'Smithie!' he gasped urgently.

'Where's the fire, Dickie?' Common Smith asked, feeling quite pleased with himself that the dodge had paid off.

But before Bird could answer, the sudden roar of powerful motors farther up the river in the darkness told both of them that their trick hadn't worked after all.

Chapter Three

Anxiously the deck crew of the *Swordfish* peered into the night, wondering when they dare start up. For there was no mistaking the angry buzz of powerful engines to their front on the river, growing first loud and then low, as the unknown craft zig-zagged back and forth.

'It's pretty obvious,' Smith said, straining his eyes in an attempt to spot the other craft, 'that they're looking for us. Nobody in his right mind would be stooging around at this time of night.'

'Exactly,' Dickie Bird agreed. 'The question now is – do we start up?'

Common Smith bit his bottom lip, a worried frown on his young face. 'That would definitely give our position away.'

'They'll find us in the end anyway.'

'Well, the estuary's broad just here and we might just slip through, Dickie.' He stopped short. A bright white light had snapped on. Now the harsh, icy beam was weaving from side to side systematically covering the river, and it was coming closer to the drifting, silent *Swordfish* by the instant. Smith knew he had to do something. But what? Anything he did now would reveal their position.

Dickie Bird made his mind up for him. 'Let's knock the light out, start engines and make a run for it, Smithie. With a bit of luck we'll pull it off, as the actress said to the bishop,' he added with an attempt at humour.

'Right, you're on, Dickie!' Common Smith cried. He leaned out of the bridge-house and yelled to Ginger Kerrigan, who was perched up behind on the monkey island, 'All right, Ginger, knock that light out tootsweet.'

'Ay, ay, sir,' Ginger answered smartly, as if he were still a leading hand in the Royal Navy. He tucked the heavy butt of the Lewis gun into his right shoulder and grunted, 'Put this in her friggin' pipe and smoke it.' Next moment he had pulled the trigger and a stream of bullets hissed glowing across the intervening water straight for the beam.

Smith didn't wait to see what happened. He whistled down the tube and commanded, 'Start up both.'

The Thorneycroft engines instantly sprang into pulsating life. In the same moment, the bright white light went out so abruptly that it left them blinking in the sudden darkness.

'Good work, Ginger!' Dickie Bird cried exuberantly. 'That's the stuff to give the troops.'

That sudden burst of machine-gun fire seemed to have worked. For the unknown craft ceased its weaving back and forth across the estuary. There was an abrupt roar of engines and it was speeding away, going all out, as the *Swordfish* edged forward very slowly at a mere five knots, for she was moving without riding lights, and there were no sound- or light-buoys in the river to guide her.

'Yon cheeky bugger Kerrigan seems to have put the wind up 'em, sir,' Ferguson commented as the sound of the other craft's engines started to die away in the distance. 'Though I no trust it. They're a cunning lot, them foreigners.'

Common Smith didn't say so, but he, too, was a little puzzled. Why all the fuss only to be frightened away in the end by a single burst of machine-gun fire?

'Rum,' Dickie commented, 'very rum. Why–' Suddenly he stopped. 'What was that?'

'What was what?' Common Smith asked sharply.

'There, there it is again!' Dickie answered and this time Common Smith heard the strange sound: that of metal striking metal. Something was knocking against the hull of the *Swordfish*. Had they struck a buoy? But if they had, the buoy would have been activated; its bell would have sounded or the light would have gone on. 'Dickie, take the shaded torch and see what that is.'

'Will do,' Dickie said promptly, seizing the torch from its clip above the controls. The hull of the *Swordfish* had long been stripped of its wartime armour-plating to give the craft greater speed. Now it was virtually paper-thin. It could be holed very easily and that was something they could do without at this particular moment.

Hurriedly he clattered down to the deck where Billy Bennett met him, saying, 'The noise is coming from the front of the hull to port, sir.'

Dickie murmured 'thanks' and hurried to the other side of the *Swordfish*. He switched on the shaded torch. It didn't give off much light but in the blue beam he could see the water around fairly clearly.

'Oh, my sainted aunt!' he gasped abruptly.

'What is it, sir?'

'Look down there – at that bloody monster,' Dickie answered and held the beam in place so that the portly sailor could see.

Now it was Billy Bennett's turn to gasp. 'Cor ferk a duck, sir – *a bleeding mine!*'

Dickie cupped his hands to his mouth and yelled urgently, 'Stop engines.' Feeling a cold trickle of sweat course its way down his spine in apprehension, he stared at the horned steel monster with its ton of high explosive which was now washing back and forth inches away from the *Swordfish's* bow. It would take just one of those horns to strike the hull and the *Swordfish* would be blown to perdition and her crew with her.

Swordfish came to a gentle halt. At the port bow, Bird and Bennett held their breath as Smith came running down to find out what the trouble was. Would the mine drift away in the gentle bow wave? Dickie said a silent prayer, perhaps the first time he had prayed since the chapel at Harrow-on-the-Hill in what seemed another age. And his prayer was answered. Slowly, very slowly, as if reluctant to be cheated of its victim, the mine disappeared into the darkness.

'What's the matter, Dickie?' Smith gasped.

'*A mine,*' Dickie Bird answered, flashing his darkened torch in the direction of the disappearing mine.

'God Almighty!' Smith said appalled. 'So that's why they were zig-zagging about like that a few minutes ago.' Then the thought struck him like a blow from a sledge-hammer. 'And they'll have planted others too.'

'Exactly.'

Smith's mind raced. He told himself they

couldn't go back now, the Huns had rumbled them. But dare they go forward? And he hadn't much time to make his decision. They had to make the rendezvous with the Dutch barge and be loaded on it before first light, otherwise the whole deception would be to no point. They'd be stalled here in the estuary for ever.

'All right, break out some rifles, Dickie. We want some good stout men with boathooks on both sides of the deck. Ferguson can see to that.'

Dickie looked aghast. 'You're going to chance it?'

'I've no alternative, Dickie. We're a lucky boat.'

'We *were*,' Dickie intoned.

Moments later they were under way once more, anxious men armed with boathooks in position on both sides of the *Swordfish*, while the officers illuminated the water to port and starboard the best they could, eyes straining to catch the first glimpse of one of the deadly mines.

The minutes passed leadenly. There was no sound on the river now save the monotonous throb of their engines and the eerie cry of some night bird.

Slowly they pushed on to their rendezvous, each man's nerves jingling with the tension of this fight with the sinister, silent enemy, the men hardly, it seemed, daring to breathe.

'There, sir!' Sparks cried, breaking the heavy, brooding silence, 'there's one of the buggers.'

Smith flashed his torch farther across the water. Sparks had not made a mistake. Coming towards them, bobbing up and down on the faint current, was one of the evil devices. 'Stand by with the boathooks,' he commanded, trying to keep a grip on himself.

Slowly, very slowly, the mine drifted towards the *Swordfish*. The deckmen tensed with their long, pronged boathooks, like medieval pikemen preparing to meet an enemy charge.

'*NOW!*' Common Smith snapped.

Two of the ratings placed their boathooks against the wet, gleaming side of the mine, taking extreme care not to touch the prongs which meant sudden death. As the *Swordfish* moved forward at a snail's pace, they took the strain.

'Secure,' one of them said tightly, not taking his eyes off the mine for a second, as Smith directed the beam of his torch onto it.

'Start the bastard moving,' Smith gave the order. 'You others get out of the way.'

Hurriedly the men on that side of the deck moved back to allow the two ratings, now holding the mine, to move.

Bracing themselves, the ratings, both sweating heavily despite the evening cold, and grunting with the effort, started walking to the rear of the craft.

Mesmerized, the rest of the deck crew stared at them and at the mine beyond. One slip, one wrong move, and they were done. They all knew.

There was no sound save that of the two ratings' heavy breathing as they pushed the one-ton mine through the water. Then the mine was beyond the bow, bobbing up and down in the slight wake while the two ratings collapsed against the rail sobbing for breath.

Common Smith made a snap decision. 'Ginger,' he called.

'Sir?'

'Knock the bastard out with the Lewis gun when I give the order.'

'Knock it–?'

'You heard me, Ginger,' Common Smith interrupted Ginger Kerrigan's protest. He flashed the torch on the vanishing mine,

126

barely visible now in the inky darkness.

'What's the plan?' Dickie Bird asked sharply.

Common Smith didn't reply immediately. He was making a quick calculation about what a safe distance was to fire at the mine. Then he said, 'Dickie, I'm going to take a chance. We can't go on like this, we'll miss the rendezvous if we do. To judge by the sound of that boat's engine, it was quite a small craft. I doubt if it could carry more than half a dozen mines.'

'Agreed.'

'So I'm hoping and praying that it laid a thin line of mines in our path. Once we're through, we're away. We're in that thin line at this moment–'

'Sympathetic detonation?' Dickie Bird beat him to it.

'Exactly. If we set off one I'm hoping the shock wave will set off the others and we'll be free from the devilish beasts.' He raised his voice, judging that the mine they had just dealt with could do them no harm now, 'Ginger – *open fire!*'

The sailor hesitated. Then he pressed the trigger of his Lewis gun and glowing lead zipped across the surface of the water towards the mine.

Suddenly, startlingly, with a great roar, it exploded in a vivid scarlet that lit the night. Automatically Smith opened his mouth to prevent his eardrums bursting as the shock wave struck him across the face like a blow.

The water heaved and writhed in a sudden white fury. Then a second later there was another tremendous explosion, perhaps some hundred yards away. And another ... and yet another.

Night was turned into day. The *Swordfish* heaved and twisted violently. The crew grabbed stanchions for support, their faces contorted with the violent shock of the explosions. Then it was over, leaving behind a great echoing silence, broken only by the steady purr of the *Swordfish's* engines.

Finally, Smith forced himself to overcome the shock of those tremendous explosions. In a voice that he hardly recognized as his own he ordered 'Steady ahead, both. Lookouts keep your eyes peeled for the barge.'

They were moving again towards that date with destiny.

Chapter Four

'I'm sorry m'dear,' the naked General said. 'I know I'm being a deuced nuisance, but I would consider it a great favour if you could have another try with me please.'

He groaned and she said, 'Of course, anything you want, sir. You're a nice person and I've got a lot of time.'

The General beamed at her, his mouth showing the yellowing false teeth which made him look a bit like a seedy horse. On his naked body were exposed all the ravages of age and 50 years of war.

There were old scars, suffered in colonial wars she had never heard about. She couldn't fathom why the General wanted her to play with him from behind and nor was she prepared to ask. She had long become accustomed to the ways of men, strange as they often were. She suspected that it had something to do with their first sexual experiences, but it was not a matter of any great concern to her. If she could satisfy him that was all well and good.

Obediently she put her hand between his spindly, scarred shanks and gently took hold of him.

'The balls first m'dear,' he reminded her, 'if you don't mind, but not too hard. I'm very old, you know.'

She did as he asked and he said with a little sigh, 'Now that is very pleasant, I must say. Reminds me of other times when I wasn't the old fart I am today. Please carry on, m'dear. You're in charge now. Keep it up!' he chuckled in his throaty fashion and she could hear the liquid in his raddled old lungs.

She was seized by a strange kind of rage which she could not define. Then she stopped suddenly and without knowing why she burst into tears.

With a creak of ancient joints, the General straightened up and turned to face her, his wrinkled features full of concern. 'What is it, dear?' he asked and touched her cheek gently, as bitter tears coursed down her face as if she would weep for ever. 'Come on, gal, spit it out! I love you, you know, and I'm your pal as well.' He paused as he hesitated to ask that terrible final question: 'Is it me?'

Blindly she groped for his skinny, gnarled hand and sobbed, 'No, of course not. You've always been so kind to me. Kinder than any man I've known.'

'Well, what is it?'

She attempted to pull herself together, wondering whether she could tell him.

But the General had already guessed. 'It's that Canadian Johnny – er – McIntyre, isn't it?'

Unable to speak, she nodded, the tears still flowing down her pale, pretty face.

He considered for a moment, a thin smile on his old, withered face. 'He looks a real man, I must admit,' he said finally. 'With him you wouldn't have to play silly games like you have to do with me. A brave man, too. I've heard all about him.' He reached for his silk khaki shirt, but she beat him to it. 'No,' he said quite firmly, for him, 'Let me put it on.'

'I'll try again. I'm sorry. I was being silly.'

He shook his head. 'No you weren't being silly. You were being sensible. I'm old and you're young with a long life in front of you, m'dear. You must make the right decisions *now*.' He started buttoning the shirt with his stiff fingers, obviously finding it difficult. But then normally his batman dressed him. 'I suppose it won't be Monte after all!'

He forced a grin and her tears started to

run again at the look on his face. 'Bloody Bognor Regis, I expect!' She didn't know where Bognor Regis was, but the way he said it, his air of final resignation, made the tears flow even more freely.

'I'll stay with you, if I must,' she said thickly.

He shook his head. 'No, m'dear, I'll be dead in a year or so, I know it. What will happen to you then? You won't get my pension, because I can't marry you.' He shrugged his skinny shoulders, 'Have to be fair on you, m'dear.'

Under other circumstances he would have looked absurd standing there with his overlong shirt dangling about his spindly shanks. There was an air of tragic nobility about him at that moment that tore at her heart. But she knew now she had made a decision. She couldn't go back.

With difficulty he pulled on his silk drawers and said as if the matter were closed, 'I'll give you some money of course and if he wants you, your Canadian, tell him to take you out of this bloody country. When we've gone, you know, the Army of Occupation, God only knows what might happen to a gal like you who's taken up with the English.' He patted her hand tenderly.

'Don't worry about it. You've been a good gal to me and what more can I expect at my age? I've had a lot more pleasure with you than a good few chaps of my advanced years. Now then, sit down a bit and have a glass of champers with me. Pass me my britches, please, dear, before you go.'

So they sat there, the aged general with his yellow horsey teeth and the pretty German girl, with tears still trickling down her cheeks, drinking their champagne in silence, each wrapped in a cocoon of their own thoughts.

On the floor above McIntyre was talking to 'C' in London, unaware that decisions were being made which would affect the rest of his life, until one day as he charged up that gravelled beach at Dieppe, a German bullet would slam into his brave heart and he would be dead. 'The Hun's aware of them,' 'C' was saying, shouting into the phone as usual, as if he thought he had to in order to be heard in Germany. 'They've made one attempt to stop them. Fortunately our chaps were quicker off the mark.'

'Good, sir,' McIntyre retorted and then, knowing that the phone might well be tapped so that he had to be careful in what he said, added, 'Did the link-up' – he meant with the Dutch barge – 'go off all right?'

'Yes, so far so good. But naturally I am not altogether pleased with the situation.'

'How do you mean, sir?'

'Well, if they know our chaps are on their way, which they do, they'll be on the lookout for them, won't they? Anything you can do at your end?'

McIntyre considered for a few moments. Outside, some drunken Tommy was singing the old wartime song, *'Goodbye … Goodbye … don't sighee…'* He remembered the infantry going up to the trenches singing that same song. Laden like pack mules they had slogged forward with the guns already thundering, knowing that most of them were going to their deaths, but totally fatalistic about it. *'Wipe the tear from your ey-ee…'*

'I'll see what I can do, sir,' he said. 'I could get a party of the lads together. Tough hombres.'

'What?' 'C' asked, puzzled.

'Hard men, sir.'

'I see,' 'C' answered, and then bellowed from London so loud that McIntyre was forced to hold the phone away from his ear. 'Do the best you can. There's something on.

We've got to stop it. We don't want another bloody war on our hands. The last show was just about bloody enough.' The phone went dead.

Slowly, thoughtfully, McIntyre replaced his phone on its cradle and looked out at the great cathedral, and the river beyond which divided two worlds, that of the Allies, the victors, who had had enough of war, and that of the defeated Germans who wanted their revenge.

He sat down at the desk and pursed his lips. From what the German girl had said, he'd guessed that von Horn now knew when the Allies would be withdrawing to the west from the left bank of the Rhine. They would pick that time to strike. But how and with what?... *And where, you fool?* a hard little voice rasped at the back of his brain.

The Weimar Government which ruled post-war Germany wouldn't be involved, he knew that. There'd be no swarm of Huns coming across the Rhine thirsting for a fight. It would be the nationalists, Hitler's lot or something similar, who would try to send the balloon up.

'Hell's Angels', that strange title went through his mind once more, as it had done a lot of late. What did it mean? Who were the buggers? How would von Horn start the trouble with them, whatever they were? He breathed out hard like a man sorely tried. So many bloody questions with so few bloody answers.

Outside, the wandering drunk was wailing now, '*M'selle from Armentiere ... never bin fucked for twenty years... Inky pinky parlez vous...*' McIntyre grinned in that tough, cynical manner of his, his problems forgotten for a moment. 'In half a mo,' he said aloud in the fashion of lonely men who talked to themselves, 'The Redcaps,' – he meant the military police – 'are gonna be after you, old buddy ... singing dirty ditties like that!'

Then he forgot the drunk and tried to concentrate on his problem once more.

He didn't get far. There was a soft knock on his door. 'Come in,' he called, a little annoyed at being disturbed when he was trying to think; thinking didn't come easily to him. He was a man of action.

It was the German girl and he could see immediately that she had been crying. He didn't ask why. It wasn't his style. He preferred not to get emotionally involved with people. It was better that way. Thus it was that he was caught completely off guard when she threw herself at him, sobbing 'McIntyre, will you have me?'

Later when she had calmed down and he had seated her opposite him and given her a cigarette to calm her nerves, she surprised him once again by giving him the vital piece of information. 'You know these Hell's Angels you've spoken about several times, McIntyre.' Even now she couldn't accustom herself to calling him by his first name, Dougal.

'Yes,' he answered warily.

'I have thought about it and have remembered something from the war when I was a little girl.' She smiled a little sadly, 'When I was young and innocent.'

'Go on,' he urged her, grateful for anything that would help him solve the mystery of these men who were, as von Horn had told the countess, 'half-Americans'.

'Well, they were great heroes then – during the war. Women used to buy their photographs in the cigarette kiosks. Things like that–'

'But who were they?' he interrupted her.

'Part of von Richthofen's flying circus.'

'Pilots?'

'Yes, the best in Imperial Germany and when the war ended they refused to surrender. They flew off to Sweden and were interned there until the storm had blown over.'

'And what then?'

'They disappeared to America, as I heard, and started performing for the *Amis* to make a living.' She looked winningly at him and added, 'I hope I've helped?'

His hard face, that looked as if it had been carved from granite, cracked into a smile, eyes gleaming eagerly. 'You certainly have. Now I know who the enemy is! I think this calls for a drink.' He took out his silver hip flask and handed it to her. 'Take a slug. Hell's Angels, we'll get you now.' Outside, the drunk had launched into *'It's a long way to Tipper...'*

'Shut up with that racket,' a harsh voice cut in. 'Or I'll put you on a fizzer. You'll be in the guardroom before yer friggin' feet can touch the friggin' ground!'

McIntyre grinned. 'Listen,' he said, 'I think you ought to be kissed, sister,' and he did so.

Chapter Five

'They were a really tough bunch of old sweats,' McIntyre told himself, as they waited there, where the Rhine flowed from Holland into Germany. All NCO's with those wrinkled nut-brown faces which indicated they had seen long service in India and Egypt. Most of them had been in the trenches in the last show and they had that quietly confident look about them of men who had survived hell and knew it.

Now they sat on the grass, watching the river flow by, puffing at their Woodbines, exchanging a few words with each other now and again, but with their eyes keen and intent. McIntyre knew why, he had picked them from headquarters for that reason, they were ready to go into action at a moment's notice; and they'd pull no punches. If they were ordered to, they'd kill without asking too many questions. For they had been brought up in the hard school of the North-West Frontier and the trenches, where the man who hesitated didn't live long.

139

Again McIntyre took out the camera and pretended to focus it on the shipping passing by. In reality the camera concealed a high-power lens with which he could survey in detail any craft which appeared suspect to him. But so far he had seen nothing that seemed out of place. It was the usual Rhine traffic, barges passing to and fro from Germany and Holland, eel fishermen hugging the banks in search of a catch, a German police patrol boat and a few daring sportsmen dodging the heavy traffic with their rowing boats. All the same, McIntyre was on his guard. The barge with the concealed *Swordfish* on board was due to cross from Holland to Germany in the next sixty minutes or so and the big, tough Canadian was quite sure that von Horn would have his people checking anything that looked suspicious coming in from Holland.

'So the old sarnt major said,' one of his NCOs was saying in a cockney accent, 'get yer friggin' plates o' meat down them apples and pears right smartish or else, laddie...!'

Suddenly McIntyre stopped listening. A barge coming from the German side of the great river, as if it were bound for Holland, had run out a series of little flags, which

McIntyre supposed meant something to the other bargees and was beginning to slow down almost in mid-channel.

'Cor ferk a friggin' duck!' the cockney was saying, 'Have a heart, Sarnt Major, can't a geezer have a crafty wank in his charpoy of a Sunday afternoon?'

Hurriedly, McIntyre focused the camera with the higher-power lens. The barge came into full view in the circles of gleaming, caliberated glass. Men were hurrying back and forth, as if the vessel was in some sort of trouble and the skipper had ordered them to get moving, double-quick time. McIntyre raised the glass and peered at the bridge, as if he might be a tourist taking snaps of a ship in difficulty.

There was the skipper behind the big old-fashioned wheel. But McIntyre knew instinctively that this was no Rhine barge skipper, the kind who smoked a pipe and kept some sort of mongrel pooch with him on the bridge. This man was lean, efficient and ruthless. With his peaked black cap set at a jaunty angle, he could be nothing less than a German naval officer.

'Hush up, lads,' he commanded, lowering the glass, as the barge came to a complete halt. 'I think we're on to something.'

141

The cockney stopped his tale immediately. At once they were controlled, wary NCOs who were the backbone of the British Army. Without being ordered to do so, the cockney sergeant and his mate, a rawbone Scot with hands like steam shovels moved back to the civilian truck which housed the fearsome weapon they had brought with them – just in case.

'What do you think, Sir?' Ramsbotham, a big, bluff sergeant major in the West Yorkshire Regiment, and the detachment's most senior NCO, asked.

'Don't know, exactly, Sarnt Major,' McIntyre replied. 'Something smells though. Why has the barge stopped so suddenly? Seemed to be making out all right up to now. And if you look at her aft, the engine's working OK. You can see the ripples her screws are making at lower power.'

Ramsbotham nodded his understanding. 'Another thing, sir, I've just noticed.'

'What's that?'

'All the German traffic's making a wide berth around her, as if they want to get out of her way. Perhaps they've been ordered to do. Cunning buggers, the Huns.'

McIntyre saw what the grizzled sergeant major meant. The other German barges *were* making sure that they didn't get anywhere near the craft and there was no obvious evidence of why they were doing so – unless someone had ordered them to keep out of the way. McIntyre flashed a look at his wristwatch. The Dutch barge, carrying the *Swordfish* concealed in its hatches, should be coming along soon. The anchored barge with that keen young skipper in the wheelhouse seemed the obvious choice to be watched. Soon the crunch might come and he wanted to be ready for it when and if it did.

'All right, Sarnt Major, tell the lads to stand by with – well, you know what – just in case.'

Ramsbotham straightened up immediately and was about to bring up his hand to salute when he remembered he was wearing civilian clothes and couldn't. He grinned a little sheepishly and walked back to the truck where the other two waited.

Time passed. Every now and again, pretending to be a typical rubberneck watching the world pass by, McIntyre made as if to photograph the river, focusing his supposed camera on the barge when he did so. Its crew had settled down once more, but there were lookouts posted on both sides and the skipper in the wheelhouse appeared to be casually smoking a cigar but through the powerful lens, McIntyre could see his keen gaze surveying the river all the time, looking in the direction of the Dutch-German frontier. More and more, McIntyre was coming to the conclusion that this was the craft that von Horn had had posted to keep a lookout for the *Swordfish*.

The granite-faced Canadian tugged the end of his big nose. Did the Huns suspect anything, he asked himself. In theory the local river police could stop and search every barge coming into Germany from Holland, but that would hold up the whole river. So had they rumbled 'C's plan of concealment?

He nodded to the sergeant major. 'All right, Sarnt Major, send a bloke back to start up the – er – lorry,' he used the English word. 'Move it closer to the bank. If we're going to hit them, we're going to hit them fast and then do a quick bunk.'

The Yorkshireman grinned. 'We'll show the sods, if it's them,' he answered and said, 'All right, you lazy Irish git, move it up to the truck.' His grin broadened. He used the word that the Canadian officer didn't think he knew.

144

Now things began to move. A quarter of a mile downstream, where the border was, a German police boat had buzzed a Dutch barge. It circled the fast, modern Dutch craft and then a watching McIntyre could see the signal flags ticking on the police boat. They were signalling to the supposed broken-down German barge. He knew now that these were von Horn's men. What ordinary German bargee would be able to read naval signal flags? It was them all right.

The Dutch barge started to plod forward once more, the *Swordfish* concealed in her fat belly. The truck started to bump and jolt across the meadow towards the bank of the Rhine. On the German barge all was sudden activity. Her engines started up again and slowly the barge began to swing into the central stream. Her intention was obvious. The barge skipper was going to block the passage of the Dutch barge.

McIntyre grinned evilly. 'That's what you think, matey,' he whispered to himself.

The truck stopped. The two NCOs appeared once more. But they were transformed. They were clad in leather jerkins with goggled masks on their faces. In their hands they were carrying those weapons of war that had been feared and dreaded by both sides in the trenches during the Great War. Already they were igniting the ends of the nozzles. They looked at McIntyre, eyes magnified and bulging behind the masks, waiting for his signal.

McIntyre waited a little longer. The Dutch barge had begun moving deeper into Germany. On the German barge suddenly all was hectic activity. Men were bustling around everywhere and the keen-looking young skipper with his cap tilted at a rakish angle was shouting out order after order. McIntyre told himself he didn't need a crystal ball to know that the balloon was going to go up soon.

He flashed a look up and down the river. The police boat was disappearing fast up a side arm of the Rhine. It was as if the lawmen didn't want to be associated with what was soon to come. Strangely enough, the other barges had ceased coming as if there had been a hold-up farther along the Rhine. Now it was just the two barges closing upon one another.

McIntyre bit his bottom lip as the NCOs waited for his orders. He was going to have to make a tough decision – and it had to be the right one. He didn't want to create an international incident; it was the kind of thing that the radical German nationalists on the other side of the Rhine were just waiting for. They'd make a lot of propaganda out of something like that if it ever came out.

Suddenly his mind was made up for him. At the bow of the German barge a small team of tough-looking young sailors were setting up a heavy machine-gun on a tripod. He'd found the enemy all right! He swung round on the waiting men. 'Prepare for action!' he commanded.

They moved fast. Applying matches to the nozzles of their terrible weapons, weapons which even McIntyre had been afraid of during the war, they ignited the flame. A thin trickle of blue now came into view.

McIntyre took a last look at the barge through his glass. As a boy before the war he had worked on barges on the Erie back home. Then they had been coal-powered. Now this modern German barge ran on oil. If they hit it at the right spot, it'd go up in flame in an instant. Then he spotted the stains of the oil tanks. 'Midships,' he called, as the Dutch barge chugged ever closer. 'Hit her midships.'

'Yes, sir,' the muffled voices of the two NCOs answered.

'*FIRE!*'

The two didn't hesitate. They pressed their triggers. There was a fierce roar like some primeval monster drawing a sharp breath. An angry blue rod of flame shot across the river. In its path the water boiled and bubbled furiously. Even at that distance McIntyre could feel the intense heat and recoiled, holding his face momentarily. The first rod of fire fell short by a yard or two. Where it struck, the water was thrashed to a steaming, boiling maelstrom.

But the next burst from the two flame-throwers didn't miss. The terrifying, all-consuming flame struck home. A seaman on the deck where it landed was suddenly transformed into a burning torch, writhing and twisting, screaming high and hysterically like a woman, trying to beat out the fire with hands that were already flame themselves. Moments later he fell to the deck, his charred body already beginning to shrink.

The machine-gun team swung their tripod round. The little cockney sergeant didn't give them a chance to open up though. He pressed his trigger once more. Angry blue flame shot across the water with that horrifying howl the flame-thrower made. The team at the tripod was engulfed in flame at once. One man attempted to throw himself over the side into the water. He staggered a few paces then crumpled to the deck. Another managed and went under in a great gush of steaming, boiling water.

The two NCOs fired again. This time both jets struck the fuel tanks amidships. A great stream of oil flame gushed upwards. Men caught fire everywhere. Desperately they tried to fight off that all-consuming flame but their flesh started to char and crack to reveal the gleaming white bones beneath.

More oil burst into flame. Like some searing, gushing giant blowtorch the flame swept the length of the barge. It curled round the bridgehouse. The glass cracked and white paint along its wooden support bubbled and blobbed like the symptoms of some loathsome skin disease.

McIntyre caught one last glimpse of the skipper's terrified face, from which flesh was already dripping off in great black chunks. Then he was gone as the barge exploded with a tremendous roar. The blast struck the watchers, who reeled back, their clothes whipping back and forth against their bodies. They gasped for breath, as the air was sucked out of their lungs.

Debris rained down, showering land and

water with chunks of burning wood, lashing the Rhine into a fury. Swiftly what was left of the barge began to go under, while 300 yards away the Dutch skipper ordered his craft to halt for a while till the keel had disappeared altogether.

McIntyre knew it was time to go. 'All right, lads,' he cried above the gushing, sucking noise of the barge as it sank, 'let's get the hell outa here! Good show! *Move it!*'

They needed no urging. Moments later they were bumping away from the site of the ambush back onto the little country road, while in the Dutch barge the skipper signalled his craft should move on. The *Swordfish* and her crew were still in business.

Chapter Six

'We will reach Koblenz in a half an hour,' Captain Smuts, the Dutch skipper, boomed in that deep voice of his which seemed to come from that massive belly, due to plenty of Dutch beer and gin. 'By then it will be dark and we will turn into the Moselle.'

Smith and Dickie Bird nodded. It was

now nearly 20 hours since the German barge had been eliminated in such a dramatic and surprising fashion at the frontier. They had known immediately that 'C' had been behind it, and had wondered when the Dutch barge might be stopped and checked. But they had chug-chugged down the Rhine for hours without incident. It was only later that police boats started to speed by them in the direction of the frontier, still they had been left unhindered. Yet as Captain Smuts had said in his thick accent, 'We can't have luck for ever, you know, English gentlemen.'

Now as the dark shadows raced down the Rhine between the cliffs, they knew they had to leave the barge soon. Von Horn would get onto it sooner or later.

The fat, jovial Dutchman knew it, too, for he said now, as they passed yet another ruined castle high on its peak, a relic of the time when the robber feudal barons dominated the great trade route, exorting taxes from any ship that passed down the Rhine, 'We will turn into the Moselle at Koblenz. By then it will be dark. I shall douse the riding lights and unload your *Swordfish*. Then you make a run for the German-Luxembourg frontier at Trier.'

They nodded their understanding.

'Then I make a turn and sail back into the Rhine. It is difficult and dangerous without riding lights, but there will be little river traffic by that time. Your average sailorman, he will be in the inns getting zig-zag!'

'Drunk,' Bird corrected him.

'Yes, drunk and making this with the women.' He thrust his thick thumb between his forefinger and the next one to make his meaning quite clear. 'If I am stopped by the *Wasserschutzpolizei* later they will find nothing. I will tell them I am in ballast to pick up a cargo in Strasbourg, which I am.' He grinned again, '*Now.*'

He gave them what he supposed was a kind of military salute and added, 'I go and prepare the crew for unloading. We make landfall at Traben-Trabach in two hours or so.' He left them and strode away in a fat man's purposeful waddle.

Common Smith waited till he was out of earshot. The less the Dutchman knew the better, just in case he was picked up. 'His idea is good,' he said finally. 'But we'll need our wits about us. Von Horn will be frothing at the gills by this time I expect!'

'Good luck to him,' Dickie Bird interrupted. 'Serves him right. So?'

'So?' His old shipmate answered, 'I think he's got a good idea of what we're up to by now and when his creatures don't spot us at Cologne, the most likely place for us to lay anchor, he'll reason we've gone on and come after us.' He paused and watched as the Dutch skipper started to steer the big barge into the channel which led off to Koblenz on the right bank of river where the Moselle flows into the Rhine. 'Tonight we'll have to make all the time we can to reach Trier before he cottons on to us. We'll do it without riding lights and it's going to be deucedly tricky. I've had a look at the map of the Moselle, it's all bends and double bends with plenty of shallows at this time of the year while the grape harvest is going on.'

'You'll make it, Smithie,' Dickie Bird said confidently. 'All right, what's the drill?'

'As soon as we're out we make full power. At the same time, we break radio silence and see if we can raise McIntyre. I'm sure he was behind that business at the frontier. He'll know by now.'

Dickie rubbed his unshaven chin and grinned. 'If anyone's going to find out things, it's that big Canuck. He has very sophisticated methods.' He clenched his fist. 'Like punching somebody – *hard!*'

Now it was Common Smith's turn to grin. 'Come on, Dickie, let's get on with it…!'

Six hundred miles away, von Horn raged. He had just received more details of what had happened to the barge and he didn't like what he had heard. *'Eine Schweinerei!'* he snorted into the phone. 'An absolute piggery. What arrogant swine these English are, thinking they can blow up our boats on Father Rhine. Would we ever do that on their damned Thames?' He calmed himself with difficulty. 'Good, *Danke* for the message. I shall take care of the matter.'

The phone went dead.

Von Horn lit one of his thin black cheroots, puffed at it and contemplated what had to be done. By now he knew the Hell's Angels would be docking in Dordrecht within the next 48 hours. They had signalled that they had already painted US Army markings on their antiquated planes so that there would be no problems when they flew over Belgian air space to the Rhine. A former Imperial German Air Base at Limburg had been alerted to prepare to service and fuel the machines for the great attack. He guessed that most of them wouldn't survive it. But that was to the good, too. The fewer witnesses to the plot

154

the better. Still, they had to believe that they would survive. They were a hard-bitten bunch by all accounts and they wouldn't want to throw away their lives for nothing. They probably knew nothing of Hitler and his movement. But the former had promised money. So if their patriotism ran low, they would still believe they would be financially rewarded.

He took another puff at his cheroot, telling himself that soon he would be a very important man in the New Germany. But nothing could be allowed to go wrong if he wanted to achieve that aim.

Outside a strapping bunch of recruits, totally naked save for their caps and boots, were marching smartly to the swimming pool for their training. Von Horn looked at them longingly. He felt the old familiar stirring in his loins. His heart started to beat a little faster.

How he wished he could indulge himself, but he knew there was no time for that. But as the recruits disappeared around the corner of the barracks he felt happier. In the New Germany which Hitler would create, all young German men would look like those naked recruits. Hitler would put an end to the soft, effete life of the cities,

155

controlled by the decadent, degenerate Jews with their nigger jazz music and crazy art, where perverted, loose women spoiled clean young men for good.

He nodded his yellow, shaven head as if agreeing with himself. What the plotters were about was worth every risk if they could achieve that aim: a nation of brave young German men, who respected themselves and their strong, fit bodies. Then he dismissed the future and concentrated on the present.

He had guessed by now that the damned *Swordfish* of theirs was being carried by a barge. The craft hadn't been sighted since Dordrecht, but it couldn't have vanished into thin air. Besides, why had the Tommies destroyed the other barge? The answer was obvious. Right under their noses the men of the *Swordfish* were sailing the length of the Rhine concealed in a barge, probably Dutch. No German skipper, he reasoned, would take the risk.

He stubbed out his cheroot and strode over to the big map of Germany's waterways and canal system which adorned one wall of his office. During the war the system had been very useful for sending supplies to the fronts in both east and west and for transferring warships from the Baltic to the North Sea. He had always taken interest in the system.

Now he followed the course of the Rhine from Emmerich right down to Strasbourg in France. All along that length of the great river the left bank was in German hands so, in essence, there was no place where the *Swordfish* could lie up without being spotted by his agents sooner or later. So what was that damned fellow Common Smith, his old enemy, up to? And why had he come here in the first place?

He frowned and stroked his yellow skull-cap of cropped hair with long, lacquered and manicured fingers. So would they risk that, he asked himself. He knew from past experience with Common Smith and his bunch of thugs that they were no fools. They wouldn't make things simple for him. God, how he wished he had the Hell's Angels with him already. In a matter of an hour or two they could do a quick reconnaissance of the whole damned waterway system in the south. Now he would have to depend on his agents and paid informers – innkeepers, sluice masters and the like. It could take days – unless, his yellow eyes gleamed suddenly, he could outguess the perfidious English.

Suddenly it came to him with the 100 per cent certainty of a vision. *'The Mosel!'* he proclaimed aloud. 'Of course!'

He stared eagerly at the river, meandering from Koblenz on to the nearerst French inland port of Thionville. Due to the shallows and other marine difficulties the river could not be used for larger vessels. Hence there was little traffic save for the pleasure steamers that ran from Trier in summer, but they would have stopped by now. That river would be an ideal hiding place for a smaller craft with a shallow draft like the *Swordfish*.

He picked up the phone. *'Zentrale!'* he barked as the rating at the switchboard replied. 'Get me Police HQ in Koblenz.'

They had said their goodbyes five minutes before. Now, as the Dutch skipper made his dangerous U-turn in the dark, Smith spoke into the voice tube, 'Both ahead – dead slow.'

Slowly the *Swordfish* started to move forward between the dark hillsides, with here and there the yellow light of a petroleum lantern indicating that there was life out there on the banks of the Mosel.

Dickie Bird was doing the navigating, but as he said while poring over the charts with

158

a darkened torch next to Smith at the wheel, 'These charts are at least five years out of date. God knows how the current has changed the river since then.'

'Do your best, Dickie,' Smith encouraged him, concentrating on the dangerous run ahead. If they ran aground, he suspected that they'd be in for serious trouble on the morrow. For here between Koblenz and Trier the Mosel was rather narrow and the German unoccupied side was only a matter of yards away from the centre channel. The French held the occupied side here down this stretch, but Smith had no great opinion of their abilities to help the *Swordfish* if she got into trouble. The French, as he knew from bitter experience, were out for themselves.

Time passed. At the bows, Ferguson kept swinging the leaded line at regular intervals, calling out the draught and guiding the craft forward. But it was tense, nerve-racking work, especially without any running lights.

It was about two hours after they had commenced their down passage of the Mosel, passing totally silent and darkened villages, that Ginger Kerrigan, the starboard lookout, spotted the slow-moving lights on the heights to the German side of the river. He watched carefully, as the car traversed the skyline high above the *Swordfish* so that in all probability the unknown occupants wouldn't be able to see her. But once they stopped their car engine, they'd certainly hear the soft throb of the craft's motors.

In the end, as the car above them moved along at a snail's pace, he decided he'd better tell the skipper. The car was now matching the *Swordfish's* speed.

Keeping his voice low, for he knew how sound carried across water, which especially at night acted like a sounding board, he reported, 'To starboard, sir, a car, going dead slow. Wonder if they're looking for us!'

Smith reacted immediately. 'Stop both,' he hissed into the voice tube and started to steer the *Swordfish* into the shadows cast by the craggy, towering vineyards.

Just in time. Up high above, the beams of three or four powerful torches, started to search the middle of the river where they had just been.

The careful search seemed to go on for ever until finally a man grunted something angrily in German and the torches switched off. Moments later the car was moving once more and a dismayed Common Smith looked at Dickie to whisper, 'Dammit, they've twigged us already!'

Chapter Seven

Brigadier Gore-Smythe had all the trappings of a rear echelon staff officer. He affected a monocle. His boots were immaculate, as was his uniform. Tucked in his sleeve was a linen handkerchief, liberally perfumed with eau de Cologne.

But McIntyre knew he wasn't just another kind of fop, like those who had wasted Kitchener's volunteer army away between 1916-1917. One of his sleeves was empty and bore three gold wound stripes. On his chest he bore the ribbons of the DSO (with bar) and the MC. Unlike his wartime boss on Haig's staff, Brigadier Charteris, who had made all the intelligence predictions far behind the lines – with disastrous results – Gore-Smythe had been up front all the time, taking out raiding parties and mounting listening posts in an attempt to find out what the Germans were up to. More than once he had ventured from Belgium to neutral Holland and from thence behind the German lines, dressed in civilian clothes, to discover German plans, knowing each time he risked being shot as a spy if he were caught.

Now he listened to what McIntyre had to say without interruption, just occasionally stroking a hawklike nose underneath his clever, calculating grey eyes before saying, 'Well, thank you, McIntyre. As always you have done a first-class job.'

Outside the 'Dom' they were changing the guard. Orders were barked, steel-shod boots slammed down. A kettledrum rattled and the Orderly Officer shouted out the orders of the day.

Gore-Smythe smiled coldly. 'Soon, we'll be gone, McIntyre, and the Huns might well be out there in that same courtyard carrying out the same drill, though they'll be goose-stepping.' The thought seemed to amuse him and his thin, clever face cracked into a careful smile. 'But it's our job to ensure that doesn't happen, not just yet at least. We're in the middle of a slump. His Majesty's Government can't afford a war with the Hun, or so they tell us. Naturally we'll have one one day.' He made the statement quite dogmatically, as if it were a fact of life.

'Yessir,' McIntyre replied dutifully, wondering what was coming next.

His lean face became serious once more. 'McIntyre, what we are trying to do basically is trying to outguess this Hun chap von Horn and his thugs. Naturally as soon as we've left there'll be nationalist demonstrations in the big cities, Cologne, Wiesbaden, Koblenz and the like. There'll be calls for the right bank of the Rhine to be occupied by German troops once more. But the Berlin government will reject that, so what are the nationalists going to do to create the kind of fervour they need to topple the Berlin government and get themselves into power?' He peered at McIntyre through his gold-rimmed monocle.

'Pretty obvious, sir. There's going to be an incident, perhaps several of them.'

'Exactly and these – er – Hell's Angels of yours are going to be involved in it.'

'Yessir.'

Outside, the corporal of the new guard was reading out his orders to the sentry he had just posted. Suddenly McIntyre felt tired. He had been in the Army since the outbreak of the war in 1914. How often had he heard such things. Now he wondered how often he could keep on.

'McIntyre,' the Brigadier said sharply and the Canadian knew that Gore-Smythe had seen that his attention was wandering.

'Well, sir,' he said promptly, 'We've agreed on this, whatever they're up to in the way of disrupting the evacuation of the Rhineland, it's got to be done in Germany. Even the nationalists, if they come to power, won't want to have problems with their neighbours – just yet.'

The Brigadier nodded his agreement but said nothing.

'So where do these Hell's Angels come in – men who have spent years abroad so that they have no obvious associations with the nationalists?'

'Tell me.'

'They bomb one of our columns, something like that. Later on it can be put out that it was an independent action, an act of revenge perhaps, which had nothing to do with the nationalists.'

Gore-Smythe said swiftly, 'I think you've got it, McIntyre. The nationalists get their propaganda victory, rally the Hun people behind them and perhaps thus come to power. The Hell's Angels take the blame. But where? Where would they best attack our columns marching back to the Low Countries?'

McIntyre rose to his feet and strode to the

large map of the Occupied Rhineland. 'As you know, sir, the evacuation will take place down the small Rhenish country roads. We don't want the troops marching through the large cities, Aachen and the like, towards the frontier where they might come under attack from the locals. The villages of the Eifel will be quieter, so the staff has reasoned.'

'Yes, I know. But pray carry on.'

'But in the end the troops will have to converge on the bridges which will carry them into Belgium and Luxemburg. My guess is that the trouble will start there. It will have to because if it doesn't they'll be gone into foreign territory.'

'I see what you mean, McIntyre, but that's a lot of border territory to cover, even if we had sufficient planes to do so, which we don't here in Germany or from the old country for that matter either. With all this recent trouble on the North-West Frontier and the Middle East, half the RAF is out there.' He pursed his lips. 'So we've got at least a half-dozen or more border crossings where these Hun pilots could possibly strike. Tall order!'

McIntyre nodded, suddenly very grim, as if he had just realized the enormity of the task in front of them.

'Now these chaps of yours, Common Smith VC and his wallahs, what is their task?' the Brigadier began but before the big Canadian could answer there was an urgent tap on the office door. 'Come!' the Brigadier commanded.

A smart young signals officer came in, clicked to attention and said, 'We've just had a most urgent from Code S' – he meant the *Swordfish*.

'Go on,' said Gore-Smythe.

'Well, sir. The signal was a bit garbled. It's due to the Rhenish foothills–'

'Get on with it, Carruthers,' the Brigadier interrupted the young signals officer.

The latter blushed and said, 'They have successfully made their entrance into the Moselle outside Koblenz. But Code S signals that they believe they are being tailed.'

McIntyre groaned. 'Christ Almighty!' he burst out. 'This bloody operation is always one step forward and two bloody steps backwards! That Hun bugger von Horn seems able to out-think us all the time.'

The Brigadier allowed himself a wintry smile. 'Don't fret, McIntyre,' he attempted to soothe the angry-faced Canadian. 'We beat 'em in the last show in the end. We'll do the same this time.' He turned to the signals officer. 'Anything else?'

'As I said, sir, the signal was a bit garbled.' The signals officer looked a bit uneasy in the presence of the two senior intelligence officers. 'But the operator who took the message thought he heard Code S say something about suspecting a chain was being dragged across the river, something like that.' He shrugged. 'I didn't get it, sir.'

Gore-Smythe looked at McIntyre for enlightenment. But the latter shrugged, as if it was beyond his comprehension too. So they sat there wondering in silence, as outside the old guard marched, with a sergeant crying, *'Swing them arms! Remember who you are!'*

Two floors away she had found the General weeping. She had come to tell him about McIntyre. But before she could the tears had started to stream down his wizened old face as he muttered, 'Silly old fart, crying like an old Irish biddy at a wake!'

Lena's heart went out to the broken old man. Suddenly she realized that he had the mark of death upon him. He wouldn't live much longer and now she, too, was leaving him. He would die alone, unmourned and forgotten, stuck in some boarding house of that 'bloody Bognor Regis.'

She caressed his bony head lovingly and whispered. 'Come on, I'll make it work for you again.'

He looked up at her, his eyes brimming with tears. 'You don't have to take pity on me,' he said in a broken, reedy voice.

She forced a laugh. 'I'm a whore, aren't I? I'll do it for old times' sake. In the past I've done it for far less.'

Five minutes later she slipped back into his room and locked the door behind her. He had dried his eyes now and stared at her in puzzled anticipation.

She smiled at him, stroked his old face lovingly and then took off her gown. He gasped. 'I bought you those, a long time ago,' he quavered, gazing in admiration at the black sheer-silk stockings with their red frilly garters and one of the new-fangled brassieres, also in sheer black silk. 'In Paris, it was.'

'Yes,' she agreed, twirling around on the absurdly high heels so that he got the full benefit of her naked loins and delightful plump buttocks. 'And you're going to have the pleasure of taking them off me.' She wagged her finger at him warningly. 'But you're going to do it slowly. I know what a

greedy, naughty boy you are! You understand … or I'll be forced to punish you!'

His old eyes lit up. 'You're spoiling an old
man,' he said.

'You deserve to be spoiled, my dear,' she
said. 'Now take one of those garters off me,
very slowly!'

He did as he was commanded with his
trembling old claws taking in that splendid
black thatch between her legs as he did so,
his breath coming in sudden hectic gasps.

She let him wait some time before she
ordered, 'Now the other one. And I don't
want you lusting after my private parts so
eagerly. I know what you're like.'

With hands that trembled even more he
removed the next garter. 'What now?' he
asked.

'What do you expect?' she asked roguishly,
lifting up her breasts in the black brassiere.
'I know what you men want all the time.'
She tweaked her nipples provocatively.

He gulped.

'Yes, I can see it,' she said, indicating the
bulge in his pyjamas. 'You're up to your old
tricks again?'

Lena squatted above him and opened his
pyjamas, then she lowered herself slowly
upon him.

He gasped sharply, his old head twisting to one side, almost as if he were in pain.

She would have loved to have kissed him, but she knew she dare not. It would spoil everything for the old dear. She had to play the ordained game, she knew the rules. 'You must take me gently. I want none of your rough man's ways with women. You understand that, don't you?'

'Yes,' the man who had ridden against the Fuzzy Wuzzies at Omdurman with Churchill answered, feeling himself stiffen in her warm, liquid softness.

It took some time, but she didn't mind. She knew it would work for this one last time, and he puffed and panted as if he were running some great race, his wizened face flushed scarlet. Then finally his spine arched and he gave a low groan, his eyes closed, as he sought for her hand and kissed it.

'Thank you a thousand times!' he sobbed as she removed herself from him. 'You have been very kind to an old man.'

She smiled at him winningly. 'And you to me. I shall think of you always, General.'

'And I you, Fraulein Lena.' He closed his eyes and was fast asleep immediately, clutching a red frilly garter with a skinny hand.

It was thus that his batman found him at dawn the following morning when he brought in his tea and shaving water, prior to shaving the old boy.

The soldier servant took in the situation immediately: the smell of expensive perfume, the red garter and the sweat-soiled sheets. 'What a way to go,' he said in a reverent fashion as he closed the old soldier's eyelids. 'No bloody Bognor for him. Died on the job...!'

Chapter Eight

Dawn.

A thick mist floated over the surface of the Moselle, deadening the sounds the grape harvesters made as they plodded up the steep shale-covered slopes to pick the grapes high above them, their capacious wicker-workers' baskets on their shoulders making them look like hunchbacks.

The night before, as soon as they had heard the metallic rattle of chains, Smith had ordered the *Swordfish* out of the main channel of the Moselle into one of the many side streams, in this case the River Lieser which flowed from the Moselle township of Wittlich into the main river. As he had explained to Dickie, 'I once read a book–'

'My sainted aunt!' Dickie had interrupted him in that assumed, flippant manner of his, 'a chap who's read a book?'

'Oh do shut up!' Common Smith had admonished him. 'Anyway, I read that in the Middle Ages the robber barons along the Moselle used to stretch chains across the river – it's narrow enough – so that they could exact tribute from the shipmasters passing to and fro.'

'Go on,' Dickie had urged.

'Well, what they did then can be done today.'

'So you mean that the Huns have stretched some sort of chain across the river to halt us?'

'Something like that, Dickie,' Smith had answered.

Now in the dawn cold with a white mist creeping back and forth across the river, curling itself round the banks like some silent great cat the two of them considered what had to be done.

'I should imagine that the Froggies have a unit at Wittlich,' Dickie suggested. 'It's the nearest town in their Zone of Occupation.'

Smith shook his head. 'Don't trust the Froggies. Besides if we approached them the local yokels would get to know and perhaps raise the alarm. No, Dickie, we've got to go this one alone.'

'What do you suggest?'

Above them a bullock wagon was creaking its way along the heights to collect the grapes the peasants had already harvested.

'We've got to get rid of that bloody chain – by ourselves.'

Dickie looked at the white mist that covered the river. 'Well, if it is what you say it is, Smithie old bean, this is the right time to do something. The mist would cover us.'

Common Smith shook his head. 'I wouldn't use the *Swordfish*. That would alert whoever's up there. They'd hear us coming even in this mist. We need a landing party.'

'All jolly cutlasses and things!' Dickie chortled.

'Oh shut up, you daft ha-porth,' Smith snorted. 'You're in charge. Pick who you want. See the men are armed. Take the necessary equipment to break through the chain. Once you've done so, signal with your flare pistol and we'll pick you up.'

Dickie Bird snapped to attention, a grin

on his face. 'We who are about to die salute thee, Caesar!' He raised his right arm in the Roman salute.

Smith shook his head. 'You're incorrigible, Dickie! Get on with it, will you.'

Five minutes later, Dickie, Billy Bennett and Ginger Kerrigan were on their way, advancing down the path which led from the river Lieser back to the Moselle and vanishing into the mist almost immediately.

Above them they could hear the chants of the vineyard workers as they laboured at their back-breaking task, balancing on the shale cliffs and tossing bunches of grapes into the great wicker baskets on their shoulders. Once, the mist lifted for an instant and Ginger, looking upwards at a group of women pickers, exclaimed, 'Strewth, them women ain't wearing no drawers! Look yer can see what they had for breakfast!'

'Some tarts ain't got no shame,' Billy Bennett said solemnly, 'Talking o' breakfast, I could just go a bacon sandwich with–'

'Shut up!' Dickie said firmly, as the mist came down again and the women without drawers vanished.

But the path along which they marched remained thankfully empty. With a bit of luck on their side, Dickie told himself, they'd get the job done without being spotted and be on their way again as quickly as possible.

Now they were moving along the old towpath running the length of the Moselle, one which had been used in the 19th century by the dray horses which had towed barges in those days. It, too, was empty. But now in the cold dawn air Dickie could smell the pungent odour of cheap Continental tobacco. Up ahead of them there was someone, but whether foe or friend he didn't know.

Suddenly Ginger, who having the keenest hearing, was up front, crouched and turning held his forefinger to his lips. Almost noiselessly, he mouthed the words, '*Somebody ahead!*'

Dickie nodded his understanding, reached into his right-hand pocket and clicked the safety off on his pistol. He gestured forward with his hand and they moved off once more, each man at a crouch, nerves tingling at the possibility of impending danger.

The mist was as thick as ever, so thick that they almost stumbled over the civilian who was seated on the bench, moodily puffing at a cigarette like a man who was very bored and would have been only too glad to be back in a warm, comfortable bed. They stopped abruptly, startled at the sight of the man. But he continued to puff away at his evil-smelling, cheap cigarette. Obviously he had noticed nothing.

Dickie's mind raced for a moment as he peered at the civilian through the wavering milky-white mist. He was a big fellow, too big for Ginger to tackle alone. He turned to Billy Bennett who was behind him. He didn't need to say anything. Billy knew what had to be done. He stuck up his thumb and smiled. Dickie nodded and moved aside on the sandy towpath.

Noiselessly for such a heavy man, walking on the side of his feet to muffle any sound that he might make, the big Londoner edged his way forward, trying to come round to the rear of the man on the bank. Still the German civilian continued to smoke his cigarette moodily. Perhaps he was half asleep. Dickie Bird prayed he was.

Billy inched his way forward. He knew what he was going to do. He'd grab the man by the throat from behind and choke him before he had a chance to shout. He reasoned there'd be others watching the chain across the river, which couldn't be far away.

Suddenly, startlingly, the man on the bank

dropped his cigarette into the sand and commenced stubbing it out with his right foot. It was then that he became aware that he was not alone on the towpath. '*Was machen Sie–*' he began as he caught sight of the shadowy outline in the mist.

His question ended in a sudden groan, as Billy Bennett launched himself at the German.

But that sudden discovery had prepared the civilian for the attack. He was flung to the floor by the impact, but he had the wits to throw a wild, desperate punch which caught Billy on the jaw. Billy was caught off guard. He fell to his knees. The German civilian grinned evilly. He thrust out his cruelly nailed boot, hard. It slammed into Billy Bennett's chest. 'You dirty bugger,' he exclaimed and then he went wild and grabbed the German by his long hair. Before the man could react, Billy had slammed his face against the rocky bank. Blood spurted everywhere as the German's nose shattered. Billy did it again. His temper had got the best of him. He wanted to kill.

Frantically the German writhed and wriggled, trying to free himself, but Billy didn't give him a chance. He slammed the man's head down once more. Now the towpath was splattered with the German's blood, and he was weakening by the second.

Ginger came up. 'Finish the poor sod off,' he whispered.

Billy nodded, his plump face lathered with sweat. He gasped and then with his remaining strength he cracked the German's forehead against the rock. Bone splintered. The German gave a low moan and his body went limp. Billy shook him like a dog might a dead rat, but he was dead all right.

Groggily he rose to his feet, beads of sweat glistening in his thick eyebrows. Ginger grabbed hold of him. 'It's all right, old son,' he whispered. 'All right. It had to be done. Look at the cannon in his pocket.' He pulled out the big Mauser and showed it to Billy. 'He was one of them all right.' He looked appealingly at his old shipmate, swaying wildly as if he might fall to the ground again. *It's all right!*

Billy nodded and said in a weak, faint voice for such a big man, 'But it's a terrible thing to kill somebody in that way.'

'Forget it,' Ginger said reassuringly. 'He's only a bloody Jerry.'

Dickie Bird, listening, shook his head, but then he told himself that was the only attitude to take. If you didn't in their business, you'd go mad.

They moved on, each man with his automatic in his right hand now, for they guessed von Horn's men wouldn't leave the chain across the river totally unguarded. They could expect trouble and would probably get it.

Dickie moved into the lead, leaving a shaken Billy to bring up the rear. Above them in the mist, the women pickers were singing, *'Oh Mosella'* in hard, cracked voices like women who had to sing to keep their courage up. *'Schon ... und gut...'*

Suddenly Bird held up his hand.

They stopped immediately.

To their front, perhaps a yard or so away, a stake had been driven into the ground. Attached to it was a thick, steel chain, dripping with moisture from the mist. They had found it. This was the obstacle intended to stop the *Swordfish*.

He looked at the other two behind him. They nodded. He didn't need to give any orders. They knew what to do.

While Dickie Bird covered them with his pistol, they brought out the sharp, steel saws which they had carried in their packs. Cautiously they started to saw through the stake, easier than the steel which they had anticipated. All the same it seemed to an anxious Dickie, peering into the swirling, damp mist for the first sight of the enemy, that they were making one devil of a racket.

Still the two ratings sawed away with the dogged patience of men who knew their time was limited – one day they would run out of luck – but who were prepared to risk their lives for the miserable pittance that 'C' paid them and for the sake of the 'Old Country', as they always called a land which had not done very much for them.

Slowly the stake started to creak as the wood gave. Bird felt sweat trickling unpleasantly down his spine. God! Surely the racket they were making could be heard in bloody Berlin itself!

Now the stake started to break. In a few moments the two of them would have broken through it completely. Already the steel chain was beginning to sag. Dickie Bird reached for his signal pistol.

'Won't be long now, sir,' Ginger grunted and with an attempt at humour added, 'As the actress said to the bishop.'

But as Dickie reached for the brass signal pistol to signal to a waiting Smith on the *Swordfish*, to their front there was the stamp of boot. *'Was ist denn hier los?'* a harsh voice cried *'Wo bist du, Hans, du faules Schwein?'*

Dickie reacted instinctively. He fired the signal pistol in the direction of the unseen speaker.

Scarlet flame stabbed the mist. Someone screamed shrilly, as the flare exploded. *'Gott in Himmel!'* the voice began and ended abruptly.

For an instant Dickie Bird caught a glimpse of a figure staggering in the mist as the phosphorus flame enveloped him. Then all hell broke loose. Firing started every- where and in the distance he could hear the *Swordfish's* motors start up with a throaty roar.

The three men crouched low, pumping shot after shot across the river from where the firing came. A couple of times they heard yelps of pain. Once they heard a great splash as presumably one of the enemy fell in the water, wounded or dead, they neither knew nor cared.

The sound of motors grew louder and louder. 'Here comes the jolly old *Swordfish!*' Dickie Bird cried out jubilantly.' Hold on, chaps, it won't be long–' He broke off. A figure loomed out of the mist with what looked like a sub-machine-gun tucked under his arm.

Dickie didn't give him a chance to use it and snapped off an unaimed shot. He was lucky. The man reeled back as if punched by a fist, dead before he hit the ground.

Now they could hear more and more of them coming down the tow-path, an angry bellow in German obviously urging them on to the attack.

'Pull back!' Dickie ordered. 'Off you go, Billy – and then you, Ginger.'

They began to move to the rear, now firing controlled shots up into the mist, knowing they were running out of ammunition. It wouldn't last much longer.

There was the angry chatter of a sub-machine-gun. Angry scarlet flame stabbed the mist. Slugs whined off the rocks all about them. Dickie realized that time was rapidly running out for them. Where was the *Swordfish,* dammit?

The attackers pushed home their drive. Slugs howled off the shale and rock to both sides of them, and Billy Bennett yelped with pain as a razor-sharp sliver of rock lanced into his right arm. He staggered and for a moment Ginger thought he had been badly hurt. 'Billy, are you–' he began anxiously, but next moment he was reassured as Billy

Bennett grunted, *'Rotten Jerry bastards!'* and loosed off a whole magazine at the shadowy figures emerging from the mist.

Dickie Bird, listening desperately for *Swordfish*, knew they'd be overrun in moments. The time to make a decision had come. He made it. 'Into the water!' he cried above the angry snap-and-crack of the firefight.

'But I can only do the duck-paddle sir!' Ginger protested fearfully.

'Well, ferkin' well duck-paddle,' his old shipmate Billy snarled, his normally placid temper roused by the burning cut in his right arm. He didn't hesitate and dropped from the towpath into the freezing water of the Moselle. Hesitantly Ginger followed while Dickie Bird loosed off shot after shot to left and right.

A moment or two afterwards he was in the water too, as their unknown attackers recovered from his salvo and started to move forward once more. He grabbed hold of Ginger, who was having trouble, and towed him by means of his collar as he struck out for the central channel, the roar of the *Swordfish's* engines growing ever louder. Next to him Billy Bennett gasped, 'We're making it, sir! Nearly there now!'

In that moment, the rowing boat creaked out of the fog, armed men balanced in it, peering down at the three of them splashing through the water. *'Da sind sie,'* a harsh voice snarled in triumph, *'Los!'*

The rowlocks squeaked and the boat headed straight for them with that harsh voice demanding threateningly, *'Keine Bewegung ... oder Sie sind tot!'*

Dickie Bird didn't understand all the German. But he did understand the last word all right – *'tot'* – Dead!

'All right, chaps,' he gasped with resigned weariness. 'Stop moving. They've nabbed us.'

They were prisoners.

PART THREE

Chapter One

'Holland!' von Einem, the youngest of the Hell's Angels, cried and pointed to the brown smudge on the horizon, his eyes brimming suddenly with tears. 'We're almost home!'

With lumps in their throats, some of them weeping silently, the former aces of the Imperial German Army stared longingly at the dark outline of Europe which lay before them as the fast freighter ploughed ever nearer to Dordrecht. Once they had fled the Continent rather than surrender in disgrace as members of a beaten army. They had been in exile for years. Now they were returning in an attempt to restore the greatness of their old country.

Hauptmann von Pritzwitz came up from his cabin, followed by the captain's steward bearing a silver tray with glasses and a bottle. He nodded to the German steward; *'Los,* Hans' he commanded. He looked at his pilots and barked in his harsh East Prussian *'Kameraden,* I'd like you to join me in a toast.' He waited till the steward had filled the glasses.

'It's schnapps,' he announced somewhat proudly, as each of his comrades accepted a glass. 'The only bottle I could find in New York. I saved it for this moment.'

Those who had been weeping wiped their eyes and looked at the contents of the glasses eager to savour the almost forgotten flavour of schnapps.

Hauptmann von Pritzwitz raised his glass to his lips, arm set at a 45-degree angle as the old Prussian Army regulations had once prescribed. *'Kameraden,'* he barked, 'to the New Germany, *Prost und Ex!'*

'To the New Germany!' they yelled as one and then downed the fiery schnapps in one swift gulp as their commander had ordered. Next moment as tradition demanded their glasses shattered on the deck for in this manner they would have good luck.

The *Hauptmann* wiped his mouth. 'I shall tell you this comrades,' he commenced, but stopped short when he heard the soft whirr coming up to the freighter from behind. He flashed a look upwards.

A bright, silver object had appeared out of nowhere in the September sky as if by magic. Now it was heading purposefully for the freighter.

'In three devils' name's,' von Einem exclaimed. 'An airship!'

'Yes and a British one to boot,' the *Hauptmann* added in sudden alarm, 'look at the damned markings!'

They nodded in agreement. There was no mistaking those red, white and blue roundels of the RAF. They had seen them often enough in the war when their Circus had dropped out of the sky to tackle the men of the Royal Flying Corps.

'What are we going to do, *Herr Hauptmannn?*' von Einem asked urgently, as a basket began to be lowered by steel hawser from the silver belly of the airship. That would be the observer coming down to have a closer look at the freighter.

Hauptmann von Pritzwitz did some quick thinking. They were almost in Dutch coastal waters, so couldn't make any attempt to down the gasbag now, it might compromise the whole vital mission. 'Wave,' he commanded. 'Smile, look happy. Look as if we don't have a care in the world. *Los!*' Like a lot of village idiots his aces started to wave at the airship, maniac grins spread over their faces.

Now the observer was directly above

189

them, perhaps only 40 or 50 metres above their heads. They could see him quite clearly, encased in his wickerwork basket, surveying the freighter through his binoculars.

'*Shit on the shingle!*' the *Hauptmann* cursed suddenly, as he remembered the Sopwith Camels on the aft deck. American markings. They had uncrated them the day before, ready to fly from Dordrecht to Limburg. The Tommy couldn't help but see those wartime planes. The question was what would he make of them? *Hauptmann* von Pritzwitz bit his bottom lip in angry frustration.

Up in the observer's tower, young Flying Officer Higgins kept his head as he spotted the planes lashed down on the aft deck. He had found the Hun all right, there was no denying that. Still, he had orders not to arouse any suspicion, so as he gave the signal to have himself hauled back up to the airship he waved frantically to the men below as if he was saying goodbye to some very old friends.

Minutes later as the airship sailed away noiselessly along the Dutch coast and the freighter disappeared, the RAF morse operator was already tapping out his signal to that mysterious rabbit-warren in Queen Anne's Gate, London, which housed the headquarters of 'C's secret organization.

'It's all falling into place,' Gore-Smythe said to McIntyre.

Outside, they were rehearsing for the General's funeral. McIntyre could hear the clip-clop of the horse's hooves, with the riding boots set in the stirrups back to front, accompanied by the solemn beat of the muffled drums. Behind came a small detachment of infantry with their arms reversed.

McIntyre frowned. She had told him what she had done and now he didn't know whether to be jealous and angry, or sorry. He dismissed the dead general and concentrated on what Brigadier Gore-Smythe was saying. 'We know where these Hell's Angel chappies are. We know the kind of aircraft they use and we can guess the nationalists are going to use them to bomb our installation and people when we start the withdrawal from the Rhineland. All that we don't know, McIntyre,' the Brigadier added, 'is *where* exactly they are going to carry out the deed.'

'Yessir,' McIntyre said routinely.

191

Outside, the military band had struck up the solemn music of the Death March. McIntyre had heard it often enough since 1914, but the music always sent shivers down his spine.

'Now,' Gore-Smythe said, as if he had not noticed anything. 'What do you hear from Common Smith and his people?'

'Nothing, totally nothing, sir,' McIntyre answered in his blunt colonial manner.

'What do you mean?' the Brigadier demanded. 'I thought you were in touch by radio.'

'We were, sir. Ever since the barge dumped the *Swordfish* at Koblenz, we were getting regular signals. Then suddenly – *nothing.*'

The Brigadier looked worried. 'What do you make of it?'

'I don't know exactly,' McIntyre answered. Outside a sharp voice commanded, 'Corporal, you'll follow the horse with the General's decorations on that there velvet cushion. And you, groom. Don't feed the nag before the parade. I don't want it shitting all over the place. Don't look right at a funeral.'

'Yes, sarge,' the groom answered dutifully. 'Anyhow, we're gonna have a geezer with a

192

bucket at the ready to catch any horse-apples.'

'Good thinking,' the NCO replied.

Brigadier Gore-Smythe shook his head in wonder. 'My God in heaven, the army mentality! Still, I suppose the old cherry-picker would like all the fuss being made for him. Now back to our problem. I hope this is simply a technical hitch with the *Swordfish*. You know how unreliable these modern gadgets like the telephone and radio are. All the same I think it might be wise if you motored down there and had a look-see. You know the form.'

'Yessir.' McIntyre answered dutifully, wondering if he did know the form. Still, his drive would take him through the French Zone of Occupation and he couldn't see many problems happening there. 'Anything else, sir?' he asked, rising from his chair.

Gore-Smythe suddenly looked oddly embarrassed. 'The woman, McIntyre?' he spluttered. 'The young German woman. You know.'

'I know, sir. What about her?'

Gore-Smythe hesitated. 'There's the General's family. I believe he has a couple of nieces or something like that still. He was very old,' the Brigadier was stuttering now.

'If they should come to the funeral ... and of course the C-in-C will be there. That's his duty naturally. I mean—'

'You mean, sir, what are we supposed to do with her?' McIntyre cut in.

For once Gore-Smythe was grateful for that typical colonial bluntness which didn't go down well in the Regular British Army. 'Yes,' he answered simply.

'I'll take care of her, sir,' McIntyre said.

'Oh, jolly good show, Major! Jolly good.' Gore-Smythe breathed a sigh of relief. 'Well, that's about it, isn't it?'

'Yes, I suppose it is, sir,' the big, tough Canadian replied, realizing that at this moment he had made the kind of commitment he had never made before. The days of killing, walking around with a revolver in his pocket, murder in his heart, were about over. He had become a human being again, forgetting that life wasn't a trench raid when your life depended upon split-second decisions and that it wasn't all kill or be killed. 'Yeah,' a hard voice at the back of his brain snarled cynically, 'from now onward, Dougal, it's gonna be polite chit-chat and drinking yer friggin' China tea with yer little pinkie out.'

She was waiting for him in the great

lounge of the 'Dom Hotel'. A few of the younger officers were eyeing her over their glasses of Pimms, but she took no notice of them. Her days of catering to the needs of young officers for von Horn's purposes were over. Besides, her ears were still full of the sombre, sad notes of the Death March.

She saw him coming and said, 'Are you ashamed of me?'

He shook his head and took a crumpled packet of Capstan out of his pocket. 'No,' he answered, 'we're all whores in our own way. At least you didn't kill men, except this one.'

Her eyes brimmed with tears and instinctively he gripped her hand with unaccustomed emotion for him. 'I didn't mean it like that,' he said. Then he made his decision. 'I've got to go away.'

She started.

He shook his head. 'Not for good,' he reassured her hastily. 'Just for a little while.'

She saw by the look on his tough, hard face that he wasn't going to talk about it any more. 'You be careful,' she warned him.

'Natch,' he said, breathing out blue tobacco smoke. He forced a grin. 'Mrs McIntyre's handsome son wants to live a few more years, you know.'

They lapsed into silence and he knew he

had to break it soon and tell her what was in his mind.

'So the Duke of York, and you know he damn well stutters, poor chap,' one of the languid officers at the bar was saying to his companion, 'said to this chap he was going to give the DFC to at the investiture, "I heard you shot down one Fokker." And the flying type said, "No sir. It was two Fokkers I bagged, sir."'

'And the Duke of York said, 'Well you're only going to get one f-f-f-okking medal all the same."'

His companion guffawed and stroked his moustache. 'Jolly good, Archie, you can certainly tell 'em.'

McIntyre frowned. He didn't like that kind of talk. He took her dainty hand in his great hard paw and snapped. 'Got something to tell you.' There was something almost angry in the way he said the words.

'Yes?'

Suddenly he felt strangely hesitant. 'Well,' he began, 'er, when I come back–'

'Yes?' she tried to help him.

'Do you think you … and … me could get together? I know I'm not much of a catch. But I've got a job and I suppose I'll get–'

To the surprise of the two officers at the bar, the German girl suddenly put her arms around the tough-looking Canadian officer in his untidy uniform and kissed him.

'I say, old chap,' the one who had told the joke about the poor, stuttering Duke of York exclaimed, 'Rum lot these colonials.'

Chapter Two

Common Smith was sorely perplexed. He had cruised around for the last ten minutes and had discovered exactly nothing, save that the chain across the Moselle had been broken through. Of course, he had heard the firing earlier on, even Ferguson, who was pretty deaf had, remarking, 'I hope Mr Bird hasn't run into too much trouble, sir, ye ken.'

Smith 'kenned' well. The three members of the *Swordfish*'s crew had run into trouble, more than they had probably bargained for by the looks of it.

'Stop both,' he ordered down the voice-tube, adding, 'Everybody please be silent.' As the engines stopped, he and the rest of the crew strained their ears, at the same time peering through the milky white mist for any sign of Dickie Bird and the other two men.

'Nothing!

'What d'ye make of it, sir?' Ferguson finally broke the tense silence.

Smith pulled a face, his brow creased in a worried frown. 'Frankly I don't bloody well know, Chiefie. Obviously Mr Bird's party ran into some sort of bother. But what it was and where they are now, I don't know.'

'Well, sir,' Ferguson said in his slow, deliberate manner, 'They canna have gone very far. And if ye can see yon slope,' he indicated the vines in serried ranks up the left bank just visible through the mist, 'whoever took Mr Bird and the lads wouldn't get up there quick.'

Smith nodded his understanding. 'Take your point, Chiefie. So they're going to be down here along the bank of the Moselle.'

'Ay, that's my thinking, sir,' Ferguson agreed, adding. 'Course they might have pushed 'em under the water.'

'For God's sake!' Smith exclaimed. 'Chiefie, you are a real ray of sunshine, I must say.' He made up his mind, bent down to the voice-tube and ordered. 'Both ahead

– dead slow.' As the *Swordfish* started to move again at a snail's pace, he said, 'Chiefie, every man on watch now. I want every building, on both banks that we come across, checked. Clear?'

'Ay ay, sir.' Ferguson, creaked away to carry out his orders.

Slowly the *Swordfish* proceeded down the foggy Moselle, with every man on deck straining his eyes in an attempt to spot the missing men. But this part of the river seemed strangely devoid of human activity, Smith reasoned, because it was too steep for houses to be built there. Still, Ginger and Billy couldn't have vanished into thin air in the short time after the firefight had ceased.

The *Swordfish* passed under a stone bridge and as they did so the mist cleared. Then he saw it. A cart of the kind the grape-pickers used, pulled by a great, lumbering ox, with a small dog yapping at its tail to make it move more quickly.

But it was not the ox that caught Smith's attention before the mist closed in once more. It was the three men trussed and bound among the litter of wickerwork baskets on the cart. 'It's them, Chiefie,' he called down to the deck excitedly, 'Mr Bird, Ginger and Billy!'

His shout had raised the alarm, for suddenly the white mist was stabbed a blood-red and a volley of slugs howled off the *Swordfish's* hull.

They, too, had been spotted.

Smith did some quick thinking. In a way, he reasoned, the three prisoners were hostages. Their captors could kill them at will. How was he going to free them without fatalities? Then he saw the opportunity he had been looking for. Ahead of him the river curved and then did a broad U-turn, leading back to where he had spotted the ox-cart. He bent and spoke into the voice tube. 'Full power,' he commanded.

The *Swordfish* sped ahead, leaving behind the snap-and-crack of small-arms fire. At nearly 30 knots the little craft sliced through the turgid brown water.

Smith waited. Then they were round the bend in the Moselle, heading back the way they had come. He knew he was taking a terrible risk, but he knew, too, this was the only way to save Bird and the other two. 'Slow ahead,' he ordered. 'Easy now. Run her aground.'

There was a gasp from the engine room.

Smith overheard it. He repeated his orders. 'Run aground. Nice and gently now. Don't want to bugger up the hull.'

The *Swordfish* hit the bank and Smith caught hold of a stanchion just in time. They had run aground in shallow water. He knew instinctively from long experience that no serious damage had been done to the craft.

He jumped over the side and the water came up to his knees. He flashed a glance at the *Swordfish*. No problem there as far as he could see. Moments later he was clambering up the slippery slope, revolver already in his hand. Behind him, panting a little, came CPO Ferguson and half a dozen of the crew. They'd guessed without orders what Common Smith wanted to do. Tracer fire zipped over their heads. Someone was manning Ginger's Lewis gun. They ran across the soggy field. Ahead they could hear the creak of the wooden wheels of the ox-cart with its prisoners. Smith prayed like he had never prayed before that Bird's captors had not realized – yet – what he was about.

They charged through the mist. Up ahead the cart had ceased moving. Smith could hear confused shouts in German. He grinned. 'Serve yer bloody right,' he gasped to himself.

A bullet howled off a rock to his left. But

it was ill-aimed and wild. He reasoned that the Huns hadn't spotted them yet.

He waved his revolver to left and right and the ratings understood. They formed a rough line and moved forward again, trying not to make any noise. They could hear the Germans shouting in their usual way and Smith suspected, and hoped, that they were confused.

Ginger's Lewis gun opened up again. They could see the tracer burning its way through the mist in a lethal morse. Smith felt reassured. The hammering of the old-fashioned machine-gun would drown any noise they might make.

Suddenly, almost dramatically, the mist parted and there they were, the ox-cart with the prisoners and the Germans bewildered and not a little frightened, trying to edge their way through a narrow ravine out of the line of fire from the *Swordfish*.

Smith didn't give them that chance. He jerked up his revolver and cried in his best German, '*Halt! Hände hoch!*'

The revolver and the menacing look on his face sufficed. The Germans stopped in their tracks. Sullenly they raised their hands, while on the ox-cart Bird said in that affected and languid fashion of his, which hid the steely purpose beneath, 'I say, old chap, what took you so long? The smell of these Hun chaps is beyond belief.' He grinned.

Smith grinned back at him with relief, as CPO Ferguson lined up the surly, hulking civilians, looking at them in his hard Highland fashion which indicated that if they made one wrong move they wouldn't be in the land of the living for very much longer.

'What do we do with them?' Dickie Bird asked finally, as they started to make their way back to the *Swordfish*. 'We can't speak much of their lingo and it appears they can't speak any English.'

'Keep 'em,' Smith said. 'I'm going to give them over to McIntyre. You know what they say about that Canuck – he can make a mummy talk. We need to know the full story and I think they can help us, or else…!'

Two hours later McIntyre had sent his driver back with the car to Cologne and was seated in the tiny, crowded wardroom facing the three prisoners and it was clearly evident by the looks on their faces that they knew they were in trouble, serious trouble.

McIntyre let them sweat it out in the best

tradition of a skilled interrogator, smoking one of his cheap cigarettes slowly, staring at them all the while with a hard, unblinking gaze.

After a while, as Bird and Smith admired his performance, McIntyre took out a pair of brass knuckledusters, slipped them on his right hand and then slammed the knuckledusters into the hard palm of his other hand. Even Dickie Bird started at the noise and the prisoners now began to look very apprehensive.

Finally McIntyre spoke. His German wasn't too grammatical, but it was fluent and the frightened prisoners understood well enough. 'I'm going to ask you some questions and I want answers *pretty damn quick!*' His voice was low and menacing and the prisoners looked at each other uneasily, especially as McIntyre slapped those cruel brass knuckledusters against his palm once more and made them jump.

'All right, you work for *Kapitanleutnant* von Horn,' he said in a matter-of-fact manner.

They nodded and he gave them a hard smile, as if in approval. 'Now then, you must tell me what he intends to do, where he is going to attack our soldiers.' He looked at each of their faces in turn, as if etching their features on his mind for eternity.

One of them lowered his gaze, another fiddled with the inside of his collar as if it had suddenly become too tight for him. But the smallest of their captives, a wizened runt with a knife scar running from the left side of his mouth down to his throat, stared back at McIntyre as if fascinated by the tough Canadian's behaviour. McIntyre made up his mind. He slapped the brass knuckle-dusters against his palm once more for effect and barked at the little runt, 'You tell me!'

'Me?' the little German stuttered and blanched with fear.

'Yes.'

'But, sir, I don't know much.'

McIntyre looked at him menacingly. 'Tell me what you *do* know,' he barked.

'It's bridges. Something to do with bridges.'

Smith flashed a look at Bird. The latter nodded. It had to be the river line of the Our-Sauer and Moselle then, the look said.

'Which bridges exactly?' McIntyre said, holding up his brass-shod fist threateningly.

'I don't know, sir,' the runt quavered. '*Kapi-tanleutnant* von Horn told us to keep an eye on you, and to stop you so he could find out what you know. Those were our orders.'

McIntyre looked at the other two. Hurriedly they nodded their heads in agreement. 'That's all we know, sir,' the bigger of them said. 'Your Tommies are to be stopped before they cross the bridges leading out of Germany.'

McIntyre looked at Ferguson. 'All right, CPO, take 'em down below. I'll talk to them again when I've discussed this with Mr Smith and Mr Bird.'

Ferguson jerked up the muzzle of the big revolver. Hurriedly the captors got to their feet and filed out obediently enough, glad, it appeared, to get away from the big, burly Canadian before he started using those ugly brass knuckledusters on them.

McIntyre waited till they had gone before saying, 'So it looks as if we know now as much as we're ever going to know. It's the bridges. Whether they're just going to bomb them with these Hell's Angels of theirs, which seems the most likely option, or whether they're going to use other measures, we don't know. Now the question is which bridges are going to be attacked?'

He looked at Bird and Smith in turn, but their young faces remained blank.

They, too, had no answer to that question.

Chapter Three

The burly colonel in charge of the King's Irish Hussars deliberately raised his gleaming silver sword. It was the signal. The band began to play the regimental march 'Garry Owen!' In the crowd lining the streets, an off-duty soldier started to sing with the music. The Colonel glared at him, 'Parade will advance *at the trot,*' he called, while the German civilians stared at the British, some with looks of delight on their faces, others glum and stubborn, perhaps even sad.

The Hussars moved off in fine form, all gleaming, jingling harnesses, as their horses tossed their heads as if in tune with the old Irish jig.

Behind them the officer commanding the West Yorkshires gave his command, too. They moved off to the tune of 'Ilkley Moor Bah' tat'. Now unit after unit joined the parade, while the guard battalion and the numerous military policemen watched the crowd just in case there was any trouble at this stage of the evacuation. The British Army was leaving the German Rhineland. The long march to the frontier had commenced.

Up on the balcony of the 'Dom Hotel', where the batmen were already carrying down regimental silver, trophies and so on to the waiting lorries, Brigadier Gore-Smythe watched the parade, feeling the old sense of pride in the British Army, as the men swaggered down the street. But he was worried all the same.

Now he knew from McIntyre, who was still with the *Swordfish*, what his prisoners had told the Canadian about the bridges. But there were half a dozen bridges or more the troops would cross to leave Germany and they couldn't be watched effectively with the limited resources at his disposal. The day before, he had called London and had made a desperate plea for air cover from the Air Ministry. He had been turned down. It had been the old, old story – spending cuts and the fact that most of the new Royal Air Force was being used in the Middle East, keeping an eye on the tribes and bombing them into submission when they got out of hand. He had even asked that they send him a few officer cadets and their planes from the training school at Cranwell. They could be easily armed, he would see to it personally. Again he had been turned down flat, with a horrified, 'You can't expect cadets to carry out a job like that! What would they say in the Commons if it ever came out?'

The Brigadier took his eyes off the parade and walked over to the big wall map of the Rhineland, as he had done half a dozen times this morning. Again he stared intently at the river line, trying to outguess von Horn. But there were bridges all along the line. Some were small village structures; others, like the one bridging the Moselle at the old Roman city of Trier, were big. He asked himself angrily, 'Where would the Huns damn well strike?' He was frustrated at the knowledge that they had discovered virtually everything about the German nationalists' dastardly plans, save the most important thing of all – *where?*

Outside a detachment of light infantry were marching past at a cracking pace, their trumpets blaring a happy tune. But the sound did not cheer the Brigadier up. Indeed it depressed him in a way. In about a day's time, some of those same sharp, smart young men might well be dead or maimed because he had failed them.

Gore-Smythe smacked his forehead with his palm and cried aloud, as if appealing to some god on high, 'Where ... in the name of heaven ... where?'

It was the same problem that occupied McIntyre and the two officers of the *Swordfish* as they cruised slowly down the Moselle at Trier, heading for the Luxembourg frontier only a matter of miles away.

McIntyre had passed on what he knew of the events at the 'Dom Hotel'. The German woman had already been evacuated and was on her way by staff car to Brussels. In that way she would be safe from von Horn's revenge. And by now the three officers knew that the great evacuation had started and that the Hell's Angels had been spotted flying over Central Holland heading obviously for some field in Germany. 'Christ!' McIntyre exclaimed angrily when Sparks had brought that particular signal from GHQ and they had decoded it. 'If only we could have shot the buggers down, that would have been one headache less. But those cheeseheads' – he referred to the Dutch – 'love that precious neutrality of theirs.' He had smiled cynically, 'But, then, in the last show they made a lot of dough by being neutral. I guess they think they are gonna make more now that the Huns are back on their flat feet. But one day they'll learn their lesson. The Huns are not gonna play patsy with them for ever.'

They had ignored his outburst of rage at the Dutch; they knew McIntyre's fiery temper of old. But they knew he was right. They had enough problems on their hands; one fewer would have helped.

Trier was settling down for the night. There were still lights in the waterfront inns where on warm sunny nights they served the local white wines in gardens facing the river. But elsewhere the old city was obviously closing down for the night. Somewhere a little band was playing but its sounds were muted and seemed far off. All the same, the three of them recognized the tune which had once been a symbol of arrogant German nationalism and which they had learned to hate in the war.

'The bloody *"Wacht am Rhein"*,' Dickie Bird exclaimed. 'Even though it's the Moselle. What bloody cheek!' He looked very indignant, as if the old German drinking song had offended him personally.

Common Smith snapped his fingers

suddenly, as the idea came to him like a vision. 'Are we going to use the Trier bridges too, McIntyre?'

'Yes, we're gonna share them with the Frogs. Kind of symbolism for the spirit of the two wartime allies. Bit of bumf for the papers, I guess.' He looked at Smith, 'Why do you ask?'

'It was that "Wacht am Rhein" that did it,' Smith said thoughtfully, taking his time as he spoke, as if marshalling his ideas as he expressed them. 'What if it was one of the three Trier bridges, or all of them which was the target? It'd cause a sensation. Ancient Roman Imperial city and all that.'

McIntyre rubbed his jaw. 'By Christ, Smithie, you might be onto something there. Trier the largest crossing point and all people who live close to a border, as they do here in Trier, hate their foreign neighbours. Those bridges might just be the ones!'

For a while they were silent as the *Swordfish* chugged down the slow-moving Moselle, the sound of the drinking song dying away in the distance. Finally, Dickie Bird said, 'Well, if your guess is right, Smithie, what are we going to do about it, old chap? Remember, we're surrounded by Huns on both sides of the river. Tricky, you know!'

The other two nodded their agreement, both of them wondering if Common Smith had finally come up with a solution to their problem. Then Smith said, 'We could let one of those Jerry prisoners escape. Ginger could play the drunken guard – which doesn't come hard for him.'

'And then?' McIntyre demanded.

'We can see where he runs to.'

'Why?' the Canadian asked.

'Well, if he stays here and contacts von Horn, it could well mean that one of these Moselle bridges is going to be the target and he's under orders to keep an eye on it, now that we know more.' He frowned a little. 'It seems to me the only way to force the issue under the present circumstances. What do you think?'

As darkness finally fell over the old city, they considered hard. 'But how do we know he wouldn't tumble to what we're about?' McIntyre asked.

'You're going to play your hard-man act again,' Smith answered. 'Ginger, obviously drunk, has been ordered to bring the little runt with a scar up for further interrogation. Kerrigan has to take a leak over the side and while he does, our bloke does a bunk. We'll be waiting for him on that bank over there to see where he goes and what he does.' Smithie paused and waited for their reaction.

Dickie Bird said, 'It might be a way.'

McIntyre growled without too much enthusiasm. 'Okay, let's give it a whirl. If the runt and Ginger play their parts right we *might–*' he emphasized the 'might' – 'pull it off.'

It was past midnight when Ginger staggered towards the heads, where their German captors lay crouched on the floor in the tight space that stank of urine. He gave the runt a kick in the ribs. 'All right, on yer plate o' meat,' he said thickly, breathing rum fumes all over the place. 'The major wants to see yer. You know the one.' He made the smacking noise that McIntyre had done with the brass knuckleduster when he had interrogated the Germans.

The little German blanched with fear. *'Warum ... warum?'* he demanded in sudden panic, *'ich weiss von nix.'*

Ginger gave him another drunken kick and said in his best German, *'Los,* Jerry! *Mak schnell.'*

The little runt looked at the fiery-faced, red-headed sailor, who was obviously very drunk – and dangerous, because he kept slapping his pocket which bulged with the revolver he kept concealed there.

His comrades shrugged, wakened so rudely out of their doze, and the German knew he was on his own. He had to look after himself. But he could see the Tommy wasn't in control. Perhaps this was the chance he had been waiting for to get out of this mess before it was too late. Keeping his gaze lowered so that the drunken Englishman couldn't see the look of sudden determination in his eyes, he rose to his feet.

'Forward,' Ginger said thickly and gave him a shove. They stumbled forward and clambered up to the deck. The sky was a hard velvet, lit by the cold silver of the stars. But it was light enough for the runt to see that the English vessel was just cruising along and that the bank was only a matter of metres away. He had to make his dash for freedom, and make it soon.

'Got to have a piss,' Ginger said drunkenly and started fumbling with his flies, 'and no monkey business, Jerry, or it will be trouble for you!' He stumbled wildly as he approached the railing, as if about to urinate over the side into the Moselle.

The runt acted. He gave Ginger a swift push and he bent down on his knees, cursing, 'Hey, what's bloody well going on? What's there here?' fumbling in his pocket as if he were trying to find his revolver.

The runt panicked and in fear of his life didn't give him a chance to do so. He plunged over the side and began to swim strongly for the other side, disappearing into the night within seconds. Ginger rose and grinned, just as CPO Ferguson appeared from behind the bulkhead. 'I did all right, Chiefie, didn't I? I should have been an actor chap … like that Douglas Fairbanks bloke in the flicks.' He licked his lips. 'Don't yer think I deserve an extra tot of rum for my performance?'

Ferguson growled. 'All ye deserve is a clip around the lughole, helping yersen to the rum like that!'

'All part o' the performance,' Ginger answered without rancour, and yawned.

In the shadows of the towpath opposite the *Swordfish*, Dickie Bird and Billy Bennett, who had been rowed ashore an hour before, waited, listening to the sound of the escaping man swimming towards the bank. 'Here he comes,' Dickie Bird whispered. 'Keep in the shadows, Billy.'

'Yessir.'

The two of them waited. Now no sound came from Trier. The old Roman city slept. So they waited tensely for the little runt, who thought he had escaped, to appear. Suddenly Dickie Bird nudged Billy. 'There,' he whispered.

Very vaguely they could see the little man clambering up the paved bank, shaking his clothes as he did so to get rid of some of the river water.

He stood on the towpath and shook himself again like a wet dog. He looked furtively to left and right and then out into the Moselle where the *Swordfish* would be anchored somewhere in the darkness. Then, apparently satisfied that all was well and he wasn't being followed, he set off to trudge back into the city. He would have to walk it, for they had made sure he had no money on him for a horse cab.

'Well,' Dickie Bird whispered in high good humour, for he had always had a boyish taste for adventure, 'the game's afoot! Come along Watson. There is no time to be lost.'

'Eh?' Billy Bennett exclaimed stupidly. Then he told himself that all officers were barmy anyway, everybody knew that. Together they disappeared into the night.

Chapter Four

'Silence in the whorehouse!' *Hauptmann* von Pritzwitz, his face almost purple, bellowed above the racket in the big former Imperial Air Force mess.

The excited Hell's Angels, all of them pretty drunk by now, gradually simmered down. Everywhere there were drinks and the food of the *Heimat,* the Homeland that they had not seen for years. But it wasn't the food and drink which excited the veterans, it was the fact that they were back home at last and that soon they would be striking a blow to create a new and better Germany.

The *Hauptmann* waited until finally he said, 'Tonight is not the time for grand speeches. Tonight, the time has come for pleasure and celebration, comrades. We're back home and we're going to make a party of it.'

'*Hoch … hoch!*' some of the younger aces yelled exuberantly. 'Down the collar and then bring on the dancing girls, especially those who like to dance the mattress polka,' one cried: a sally which was met by loud laughter.

'Exactly,' the *Hauptmann* agreed in his harsh East Prussian fashion. 'In our time, comrades, we have fucked everything black, brown, yellow and white, even the beasts of the field, if my memory serves me right!'

Again there was loud drunken laughter.

'But we are going to be serviced by German women once again. They may not be the pure maidens we once knew.'

'Did we ever know anyone like that, *Herr Hauptmann?*' some drunken wag yelled. 'It's so long ago that I've forgotten what an honest woman is. All I had were those fifty cent whores in the States.'

The *Hauptmann* looked serious for a moment. 'Yes, you're right, Egon. But things will soon be different.' He raised his glass of Rhenish champagne. 'Now we enjoy German women, we drink German champagne, we eat German food.' He indicated the great steaming bowls of *Kohlrolladen*, mincemeat wrapped in cabbage, in front of them on the sagging table. 'The decadent days are over. A toast to the new Germany and then let the fun commence!'

As one, their faces suddenly solemn for a moment, they cried, *'Prosit'*.

Then the *Hauptmann* gave the signal to the white-jacketed mess waiter, whose pockets were stuffed with the money they had given him to supply the night's entertainment. He grinned crookedly, showing his gold teeth. He had done this often enough during the war when the officers had come out of the line. He guessed in this new Germany, that as the East Prussian with his upper-class accent had just mentioned, there were going to be plenty of opportunities to make good money on occasions like this.

Hastily the mess waiter strode to the door, opened it and bellowed, in German, as if on the parade ground, *'Fifes and drums will advance, flags flying ... ADVANCE!'*

'Parade march!' a deep bass voice retorted.

A drum sounded and then suddenly the whole place was full of sound, as a huge woman, wearing the *pickelhaube* of the old Imperial German Army came goose-stepping into the mess, the Imperial black and white flag held rigidly in front of her, her face stern and set.

There was a huge delighted roar from the assembled pilots, for the woman was totally naked save for the helmet and jackboots and

as she raised her legs to the height prescribed by regulations of the old Imperial
Guard she left nothing about her sexual
charms to the imagination.

Next moment they cheered again, as the
fife and drum band marched in, also naked
save for helmets and boots. But here there
was a difference between them and the giant
flag-bearer. As von Einem yelled in drunken
delight, 'They've all had their pelts shaven,
comrades!'

The greasy mess waiter with the gold teeth
smiled, 'Specially for you, gentlemen,' he said
above the whistles, the wild cries and frenzied
clapping. 'Cost a little bit more. But I
thought for your first night in the Homeland,
gents, you deserved something different.'

The huge flag-bearer glared at him as she
clicked to attention and commanded, 'Fife
and drum band will halt!' Her voice was like
that of an Imperial sergeant major.

The band stopped as one and those of the
pilots who were still sober enough to think
fairly straight told themselves that the girls
with shaven pubes must be from some local
dancing group who performed annually at
the Rhenish carnivals, they were so well
trained.

The huge flag-bearer waited a moment,

then she commenced goose-stepping once more to the table at which the *Hauptmann* and the more senior pilots sat. She clicked to attention with such force that the bottles which lined the table rattled violently and bellowed at the top of her voice, 'Beg to report, gentlemen, fife and drum band all present and correct.' She paused for the regulation three seconds of the old Prussian drill manual before shouting, 'We await your orders, gentlemen!'

At the other table, von Einem, who seemed to be getting drunker by the second, yelled, slurring his words badly, 'Easy! On yer backs and prepare for action, girls.'

His not very witty sally was greeted by loud cheers from the younger pilots and suggestions on what kind of 'action', the 'girls' could expect.

For once the *Hauptmann* beamed. 'Ach,' he cried, 'the spirit of the new Germany! Flag-bearer, please accept a glass of champagne.'

'Schnapps, *Herr Hauptmann*,' the naked woman corrected him, as she reverently placed the old Imperial flag down. 'Champagne is for officers, NCOs drink schnapps.'

As she bent down before accepting the drink, her huge rump rose in the air and someone cried, 'A bigger arse on her than a ten-taler nag! Need two of us to give any pleasure to a wench like that!' But the wag was wrong.

Half an hour later the big woman was sprawled across the drink-sodden table with no less a person than the *Hauptmann* himself pleasuring her, while all around on the tables, over the chairs, on the floor, the younger pilots were doing their best to do the same with the younger women.

It was thus that von Horn found them as he strode into the smoke-filled mess, stinking of alcohol and sexual pleasure, after his long and hectic drive from northern Germany. He frowned angrily at the sight of a pilot who was lying drunk on the floor and being attended to by two of the young women.

'*Welch eine Schweinerei!*' he exclaimed in outrage at the sight. 'What a filthy piggery!'

No one took any notice of him. Von Horn didn't hesitate, he pulled the old trick they had used in the mess during the war when they had wanted to attract drunken officers' attention. He drew the pistol from his holster, clicked off the safety and fired three shots at the ceiling.

The girls gasped. One of them, doing

something very pleasant to a naked von Einem, nearly caused him a grave sexual injury with the shock of that sudden volley. The mess waiter shook his head. He knew his officers of old, but they couldn't get away with that sort of thing in peacetime. He was not going to pay for the damage to the ceiling out of his own money. The golden-haired albino in the civilian clothes, Pritzwitz, was going to have to fork out for this one. He looked like a pervert, too. He'd make him pay through the nose.

But at that moment von Horn was not concerned about such matters. He had other, much more important things on his mind.

Blinking a little as if they were coming out of a heavy sleep, the pilots sat up and looked at the naval officer in civilian clothes, wondering what in three devils' names the man was shouting about.

Von Horn soon explained. '*Hauptmann* von Pritzwitz,' he barked.

The *Hauptmann*, who wasn't as drunk as the rest, though he was indulging himself in a slightly bizarre fashion with the tall nude who had carried the old Imperial flag and who sat astride his lap, murmuring something about 'There's flagpoles and flagpoles', pushed the woman aside and snapped, *'Zu Befehl'*, 'At your orders!'

'Good,' von Horn snapped contemptuously. 'I'm glad someone has some sense around here!' He clicked to attention. *'Kapitanleutnant* von Horn, Naval Intelligence,' he introduced himself. 'Your orders have come through. I think it is time to clear the room. Get rid of these wenches!'

There was a drunken murmur of protest which the *Hauptmann* silenced with a savage look barking at the same time at the huge nude woman, 'March the fifes and drums off, flag-bearer!'

She rose to the occasion, placing her *pickelhaube* on her blonde head once more and saluting, then grasping her flag she cried as if she were a sergeant major on the barrack square, 'Fife and drum band will stand at attention – *attenshun!'*

Von Horn flinched at the noise as the girls rose from their various postures, tugging at their jackboots as if this gave their nudity some kind of modesty.

The huge blonde waited for a moment till they were ready, then she ordered, making von Horn flinch once again at the racket, 'Fife and drum band will march off. *Parade, march!'*

So they marched away, drums rattling, fifes squealing, leaving the Hell's Angels to watch with sad regret their delightful rumps disappear.

Behind them the little mess waiter closed the door and gazed at von Horn expectantly, as if he half expected a tip. He was to be disappointed. Von Horn dismissed him with the wave of his hand before saying, 'Gentlemen, the time has come. The main body of the English left Cologne yesterday. A battalion of cavalry is expected to arrive at Trier to cross the Mosel in the direction of Luxembourg tomorrow, perhaps around three in the afternoon, as far as we can ascertain.' He looked at the *Hauptmann*. 'What would the flying time be from Limburg here to Trier?'

'The stringbags are pretty old crates, *Herr Kapitanleutnant*,' *Hauptmann* von Pritzwitz answered. 'They've seen better days, but I would guess about thirty to forty minutes depending what kind of wind we had.'

The pilots, who knew what their chief was talking about, laughed.

Von Horn frowned, he had no sense of humour. 'Good,' he snapped, 'and how long can you stay over your target and then return here without refuelling?' Already another idea was forming in his devious mind of how to deal with the Hell's Angels, who would be a liability *afterwards*.

'Perhaps twenty minutes at the most,' the *Hauptmann* answered. 'Why do you ask?'

'Because if we want the incident that we do, we must make sure that the Tommies are on that bridge when it goes up.'

'I see.'

Von Horn forced one of his fake smiles. 'All right, gentlemen, I'm sorry to have interrupted your, er, little pleasures. There will be other opportunities later on for such matters. But this night I wish you all to have clear heads. We go into action tomorrow.'

Suddenly the Hell's Angels were very sober.

Von Horn nodded his shaven, yellow head slowly, 'Yes, tomorrow, *meinen Herren,* you will make history.'

Listening at the keyhole, the greasy mess waiter told himself, 'They can make what they like as long as they pay their bills!'

Chapter Five

'There's his nibs now, sir,' Billy Bennett whispered as they stood in the shadows cast by Trier's old Roman gate, the *Porta Nigra*, opposite police headquarters. 'Thought the little bugger was never gonna come out agen.'

They had followed the escapee through a silent, sleeping Trier until finally he had entered the local *Polizeipraesidium*, the police headquarters just off the railway station along the road. It was then that Dickie Bird had realized finally that the runt had connections to the top. As he remarked to Billy Bennett, 'Chaps like that, petty crooks and the like, don't go to the local men in blue unless they've got important official contacts.'

Now he could see that his guess was being confirmed. Two *Schupos* in leather helmets were escorting the little man to a waiting Opel *Blitz*, chatting happily to him as if they were the oldest of friends. It was pretty clear that he had pulled some important strings during the hour or so that he had spent in the police HQ.

'What do we do now, sir?' Billy Bennett asked softly, as one of the two fat, middle-aged policemen offered the runt a light for his cigarette.

Dickie Bird thought hastily. He guessed that the runt had had some sort of contact with von Horn. Would he know more now about what was going to happen? If he did, it was worth his while to tackle him. But there was the business of two policemen. Middle-aged as they were they were still armed with rubber clubs and pistols in the continental manner. He made a swift decision. 'We'll nobble 'em,' he announced.

Billy looked aghast. 'The bobbies as well?' he exclaimed.

'Yes, the lot. We don't want anyone blabbing afterwards.'

'Very good, sir,' Billy Bennett accepted the order in his honest, loyal fashion. 'It will be done. Do you think I could have yer hand-kerchief?'

Dickie Bird looked at the big overweight sailor as if he had suddenly gone mad. 'What?' he blurted out.

Billy repeated his request. 'Want to catch yon Jerries off guard. Don't fancy any shooting outside a big cop shop like that. Wouldn't be too smart, I'm thinking. Leave it to me, sir.'

Still bewildered, but knowing that Billy had something up his sleeve, Dickie Bird handed over his handkerchief to a grinning Billy, while opposite, on the other side of the street, the taller of the two policemen was unlocking the door of the little car. Billy sniffed the silk handkerchief and grinned. 'Smells smashing, sir.' His grin vanished. 'Get ready to back me up, sir, will you, when we're ready to nobble 'em!'

'Will do, Billy,' Dickie answered, wondering what the big rating was about.

With surprising swiftness and silence for such a hefty man, Billy darted out of the shadows cast by the old Roman gate, his body bent double. He avoided the pool of yellow light cast by the gaslamp outside the almost silent police headquarters. Still crouched low, as the two policemen ushered the runt into the little car, he approached the *Blitz's* exhaust.

Dickie Bird watched anxiously, nerves tingling, ready to move at a moment's notice, as soon as Billy gave the signal. Then he saw the rating take out his handkerchief and begin to stuff it into the car's exhaust, thrust it home hard. But still he couldn't fathom out what Billy was up to.

At the wheel, one of the policemen began to start up. The car obviously had one of the new-fangled self-starters, Dickie told himself. They were now coming in from America and Opel, the firm that made the *Blitz,* belonged to a Yankee outfit, General Motors, he believed. With their cars there was no need to crank up the engine like one had to do with British models such as the Morris.

There was a hollow groan and a soft moan. Nothing happened. Now Dickie's face lit up. He knew what Billy had done. He had blocked the exhaust. The car wouldn't start and he wanted to lure one of the German bobbies out to see what was happening. He tensed. Now he realized he'd have to jump in and support Billy Bennett.

'Damned shit,' the policeman at the wheel cursed as he opened the door of the Opel *Blitz* and got out to see what was wrong. He unfastened the leather straps which held the bonnet down and opened it. It was what Billy had been waiting for. He darted forward, still crouched low so the two Germans inside the car couldn't see him. He lifted the sock, filled with earth when he had prepared for this mission. As the policeman bent to peer inside at the engine, exposing his fat, shaven neck, Billy brought the makeshift club down hard with all his considerable strength.

The *Schupo* gave a soft, hardly audible moan and went down onto his knees, but he wasn't out yet. Billy didn't give him a chance to raise the alarm. He slammed his knee cruelly into the middle-aged policeman's face. The cop's false teeth bulged out of his gaping mouth as he went down, retching as he did so. Billy Bennett kneed him again. The German hit the tarmac, unconscious or dead before he reached it.

Dickie Bird rushed forward almost noiselessly. He knew that trouble would start if they didn't move fast. There were still lights burning in the German police headquarters.

Inside the car the runt was still talking to the other policeman. Obviously they had not yet spotted what had happened at the front of the car. Billy nodded, gasping a little. He was wearing the unconscious or dead policeman's helmet. On any other occasion he would have looked to Dickie like something out a West End farce. He pointed to the rear of the car where the two were seated.

Dickie nodded, guessing what the big rating was about.

Head bent in the dim light of the shadows, Billy tapped at the door on the side where the other *Schupo* was seated. He looked up. In that instant, Dickie crept up the other door. *'Was ist?'* the policeman asked, perhaps wondering why his colleague was crouched like that. *'Problem mit der Motor?'*

Billy murmured something.

The *Schupo* sighed like a man sorely tried. *'Ja, ja,'* he growled. *'Ich komme ja schon.'* He grasped the door handle to open it.

At that moment the runt looked up and saw Dickie. He gasped, *'Ein Tommy Schwein!'*

Dickie didn't give him any more time to sound a warning. He wrenched open the door, grabbed the runt by the collar of his dirty jacket, and pulled him out. He smacked a punch at his scarred face.

Billy Bennett was busy too. In the same moment that the middle-aged cop realized that all was not well and began to reach for his pistol, Billy grabbed him and with the back of his free hand chopped him across the Adam's apple.

The policeman's yell of alarm died in a

gurgle in his throat as he went reeling back onto the leather seat. Billy didn't give him a chance to recover. He used the same technique he had done on the other policeman, cruel as it was. He slammed up his knee. It caught the cop at the point of the jaw.

Something clicked. The *Schupo* reeled back, his neck broken.

Dickie Bird grabbed hold of the runt, pistol in hand. He waved it in front of the German's nose. 'No word,' he said, threateningly.

Whether the runt understood his English or not, it didn't matter. The muzzle of the pistol, inches from the end of his nose, told the little German all he needed to know. *'Ja ... ja,'* he quavered, terrified out of his wits. *Ich sage nichts.'*

Billy Bennett grunted and lifted up the unconscious policeman by the bonnet. He slung him inside the car like a sack of potatoes, while the runt trembled, muttering to himself and wondering what they were going to do to him. 'Can you drive, sir?' Billy hissed, 'I can't!'

'Course I can,' Dickie reassured him.

'Good.' Hurriedly, Billy went to the back of the little car and removed the handkerchief from the exhaust. 'All yours, sir,' he said, sliding into the seat next to Dickie.

Bird didn't wait for a second invitation. He started up. There were a few grunts, a backfire or two and then the engine started. Bird double-declutched and slammed home first gear. Up above, on the second floor of the police HQ, a window was opened and someone shouted, 'Don't make so much damned noise!'

Billy Bennett grinned and chortled, 'They can go and take a running – you know what, sir – at themselves!'

Bird was too concerned with the controls of the unfamiliar car to answer. He steered the *Blitz* in second gear under the *Porta Nigra,* heading westwards and down to the Moselle to where the *Swordfish* was waiting for him. Behind him in the back seat, Billy Bennett looked menacingly at the little runt and said threateningly, 'One word from you mate, and yer gonna lack your friggin' front teeth.'

The runt cowered.

Slowly they picked their way out of the old city, hoping that no one would stop them and enquire why they had two unconscious middle-aged German policemen sprawled inside the car. No one did. Their luck was holding out, but next to the runt Billy Bennett could see the man was beginning to panic, and although the big rating wasn't a very intelligent man he could guess why.

The runt had learned something very important while he had been at police headquarters. Now he was afraid that once they were back on the *Swordfish,* McIntyre would be able to squeeze out of him what he knew. Billy Bennett guessed, too, that the runt realized that if he squealed to the big, tough Canadian his life would be forfeited if he stayed behind in Germany once the Allies had evacuated the Rhineland and the new boys had taken over.

Billy wondered exactly what the little German crook knew. Then he dismissed the matter. Things like that were best left to his officers; they knew how to deal with them. That's why they went to their posh private schools!

Cautiously Dickie Bird drove the little car down the darkened, deserted streets. He didn't want to attract attention to the stolen Opel *Blitz,* though he thought it was hardly likely that anyone in authority would be around at this time of night.

He was wrong.

Suddenly as if from nowhere, two uniformed figures appeared, one of them waving an illuminated disc on a short stick. 'Halt!' the one with the disc yelled, as the other policeman unslung his rifle.

'That's torn it!' Billy exclaimed.

'Hold on to your hat!' Dickie Bird cried, carried away with sudden excitement. He pressed the accelerator down hard and the Opel *Blitz* shot forward. The policeman with the signal disc sprang to one side just in time and fell into the gutter, cursing. Next to him the other one opened fire. Bullets ran the length of the *Blitz*. Glass shattered. Then they were careering round the next corner and the firing died away.

Chapter Six

The runt was dying. McIntyre knew that. As soon as the other two had helped him into the *Swordfish's* wardroom and the big Canadian had seen the ragged, gaping wound in his back where he had been hit by the German policeman's gun, he had realized that the runt couldn't live out the night. Perhaps if they could have got him to a hospital there might have been a slim chance, but there was no hope of that. So they had patched him up the best they could with their first aid kits, and McIntyre had given him a shot of morphine to lessen the pain of his mortal wound.

Now he lay on the battered leather wardroom sofa with a stiff glass of whisky in his shaking hands, looking at the three officers in a surprisingly grateful manner. Indeed twice he had murmured, *'Danke, danke fur Ihre Hilfe,'* as if he really believe that they were going out of their way to aid him.

Watching, Smith frowned. It didn't seem quite proper. His public schoolboy sense of honour was offended in some way. Didn't the runt realize that they were only keeping him alive because they wanted to pump him about what he knew?

McIntyre had no such scruples. He gave the dying man another shot of whisky, saying, 'Drink that. Then I'd like to know something from you, and quick, because I want to get you to hospital pretty soon. I think a doctor should have a look at that – er – scratch just in case it's more serious than I think.' His craggy face broke into what was for him a winning smile.

The runt looked up at him gratefully and said weakly, 'Thank you, sir.'

Common Smith couldn't follow all the German, but he got the gist and didn't like it.

'Did you speak to von Horn?' McIntyre asked.

'Yes, sir.'

'And what did he tell you?'

'To stay here and wait for the attack,' the dying man said weakly. There was a thin trickle of dark red blood coming from the side of his mouth now.

'From the air ... on to the bridges?' McIntyre prompted the dying man.

'*Jawohl.*'

'Anything else?'

'Well,' the runt paused. The end of his nose was suddenly very white and pinched and McIntyre knew what that meant, he had seen the signs often enough. The runt had perhaps only minutes to live.

'Go on, please,' he urged. 'Then we must get you to hospital.'

'Thank you, sir,' the runt whispered in a pathetically grateful manner, 'Just in case, they're going to fix the bridge from ... the ... ground.'

McIntyre translated quickly and looked

meaningfully at the other two, before turning back to the dying man on the old ward-room couch. 'But which bridge?' he snapped. 'There are three across the Moselle here in Trier.'

The runt opened his mouth. But suddenly, abruptly, in a manner which caught them by surprise although they knew he had so little time to live, the German's head lolled to one side, mouth open and gaping.

McIntyre looked alarmed. He bent down and grabbed the runt by the shoulder. 'Hey,' he said in English, 'don't friggin' well die on me yet!' For a moment it looked as if he was about to haul back his fist and hit the man.

Common Smith snapped, 'None of that! Can't you see he's dead?'

McIntyre controlled himself with difficulty. He gave a deep sigh and said, 'Yes, I guess you're right.'

'I know I am,' Common Smith retorted. 'I'll get CPO Ferguson to have him cleared away from here. He can go down with the others in the heads and—'

'No, over the side with him while it's still dark. We don't want to scare the other Hun bastards with the sight of his body. We might have need of them yet, Smith.'

'You're a hard bastard,' Smith said. 'But I

suppose you're right.'

'In my line of business you've got to be a hard bastard,' McIntyre answered, the dead runt already forgotten as he began to ponder over what he had learned from him.

Minutes later they had weighted the dead German and dumped him over the side, then watched as the body disappeared into the murky waters of the Moselle, while Ginger had kept a lookout for any observers, but there had been none. Trier slept soundly, though, as McIntyre remarked after they returned to the wardroom to drink the usual pink gin even though it was four in the morning, 'You can guess the local law will be looking for us once they find that abandoned Opel *Blitz* and that their man is missing. So we've got to make some decisions before first light.'

Common Smith nodded his agreement. 'You're right. While you were dealing with the body I got Sparks to signal HQ and find out what bridge or bridges our chaps are going to use to cross the Moselle.'

McIntyre's craggy face lit up. 'Good thinking! That should give us a clue to where we will be involved when the time comes.'

The two officers didn't comment, but they

knew he was right. They would have to be involved in due course whatever the risk. Dickie Bird, however, said, 'But for the time being, until we know when the troops arrive, where are we going to park ourselves and the *Swordfish*?'

That stopped them in their tracks, especially as Dickie added, 'Once it's daylight and the police start searching the river – and they'll know from the dead Hun that we're here somewhere – we're going to stick out like a sore thumb, chaps.'

Common Smith frowned hard. His old shipmate was right. The Moselle wasn't particularly broad as it flowed through Trier and here there were no side-streams where they might have hidden as there had been further upriver. He looked across at the Canadian as if he hoped he might have a solution to the problem, but the latter shook his head.

Time passed leadenly as they sat in silence, drinking their pink gins and thinking, their young faces wreathed in cigarette smoke. Outside there was no sound save for the soft tread of the lookout pacing the deck, keeping his gaze on the nearest river-bank for the first sign of impending trouble. But already, some way off, they could hear the first cries of the awakening birds. It would be dawn soon. There wasn't much time left for them.

'Listen,' Smith said, breaking the heavy, brooding silence, 'What about this?'

The other two turned and looked at him expectantly. 'What will von Horn expect us to do now that he knows we know that the bridges at Trier are the target? I think he'll assume we'll get out of the city and head farther up the river towards the Luxembourg border until the trouble starts.'

McIntyre nodded his agreement and Dickie Bird said, 'Yes, that's the sort of obvious way the Hun mind works, Smithie.'

'Oh don't be a damned ass, Dickie,' Smith said. 'This is serious!'

'The Huns are too, old bean,' his friend replied without rancour.

'But let's fool him,' Smith went on, his mind warming to the plan as he thought more about it. 'Let's get even closer to the site of the trouble – that big medieval bridge in the heart of Trier.'

McIntyre frowned. 'Chancey. We won't last long there without being spotted, Smith. No place to hide.'

'But there is,' Smith exclaimed triumphantly, as some way off the great clock of

Trier's cathedral chimed five. 'Remember, as we came under the bridge there was a sort of little harbour to the right, where the pleasure steamers which ply the Moselle in summer were anchored?'

They nodded wondering what he was getting at.

'Well, if we could...' Hastily he explained his bold scheme to them, knowing that time was running out *fast* – if he was going to carry it out.

McIntyre whistled softly when Smithie had finished outlining his plan, saying, 'It might just work,' while Dickie Bird said in admiration, 'Didn't think you had it in you, old bean. Very devious. Very devious indeed!'

'So shall we?' Smith began to ask as there was a soft, polite knock on the wardroom door. 'Come,' he ordered.

It was Sparks. In his hand he held the standard buff form on which signals were written in the Services. 'Most Immediate, sir. From GHQ. I've decoded it. Thought you wouldn't mind, seeing it was most immediate.'

'No,' Smith answered and seized the message eagerly. It was obviously going to be in answer to the latest information they

244

had transmitted to GHQ Intelligence in Cologne, and it was. It was from Brigadier Gore-Smythe personally, and although it had been sent in code, the Intelligence chief was obviously not taking any chances in case the Germans had cracked the code.

His eyes skimmed the signal and then, clearing his throat, he read it aloud to the others. *'Micks are being prepared to give flyboys headache. Still keep beady eye open for ungentlemanly behaviour. Witching hour should be three pip-emma. Love. Mother.'*

Even McIntyre's craggy face cracked into a wintry smile at the 'Love. Mother.'

'Didn't think the old Brig said such things,' Dickie commented and then seriously he asked, 'Micks – does he mean the Eighth Irish Hussars?'

'Yes, they're the leading formation,' McIntyre answered his question. 'They'll reach the Moselle first.'

'So what's the headache?'

Both Smith and McIntyre thought hard at that until the latter said, 'What would give flyboys a headache? I think it is anti-aircraft fire. My guess is that the Huns wouldn't think cavalry would be equipped with anything like that.'

Dickie Bird clapped his hands together in

schoolboyish delight, 'Natch!' he chortled, 'They'll surely get a headache.' He looked at Smith. 'It looks as if we'll have to take a chance and carry out your plan to ensure, as the Brig puts it, there is no ungentlemanly behaviour.'

Suddenly Common Smith VC looked very serious. 'I agree,' he said solemnly, 'It is our duty. But remember, if they nab us we're done for.'

He let the words sink in and McIntyre told himself that although the two young Englishmen seemed to take everything in that easygoing, flippant upper-class manner of theirs, they were as hard as steel beneath that front. When the chips were down, they were prepared to sacrifice everything. Aloud he said, 'All right, Smith, I'm prepared to take the risk.'

Smith hesitated no longer.

Five minutes later they were heading back upstream right into the heart of Trier, while outside the first of the city's blue trams, taking the workers to their factories, began to clatter by along the opposite bank.

The decision had been made. The die was cast. Now everything lay in the hands of fate.

Chapter Seven

Major Digby-Watham of the King's Royal Irish Hussars came galloping down the mountain track high above the Moselle, crying to the troopers washing or preparing their breakfasts on both sides, 'Make way! Make way! Got to speak to the CO urgently!'

The 'Micks' grinned for the most part, a couple shouting to one another as he clattered by on his splendid charger, his luxuriant moustache streaming in the breeze, 'Yon's a mad bugger, that he is.' Then they turned their attention to the line of Khaki-coloured lorries which were following him, groaning in first gear up the steep incline to the heights.

The Eighth Hussars had been on the march two days now. As the vanguard of the withdrawing forces they had stuck to the back and side roads, looking for anything suspicious that might cause trouble for the following infantry. They had followed the course of the Rhine first, crossed the

Moselle at Koblenz, where the two rivers met, and were now making their way down the eastern bank of the river to Trier where they would cross the Moselle once again before moving into nearby Luxembourg.

Major Digby-Watham, who was in charge of the rear echelon, had exciting news for the CO and he was intent on getting it to him before the Regiment set off once again.

The CO was sitting outside his little tent on a camp-stool drinking bottled coffee laced with rum, as was his morning habit, and smoking a battered old pipe. As the dashing Major reined in his sweat-gleaming charger, he told himself the Colonel looked for all the world like one of his forefathers who had led the Regiment at the Charge of the Light Brigade nearly a hundred years earlier.

Slowly the CO, took his pipe out of his mouth and said, 'Shouldn't ride a horse at the gallop first thing in the morning, Jumbo. You ought to know that. Not good for 'em.'

The Major wasn't put out. As he slid from the saddle, he countered, 'Had to, sir. Urgent news. Had to get to you top speed.'

The CO gestured to his servant with the stem of his pipe. 'Another stool and a gunfire for the Major, Fitzgerald, there's a good chap.'

'Yes soor,' Fitzgerald replied in the accent of County Sligo.

A moment later he was back with the two items and Digby-Watham sat down immediately, as behind the heavily laden lorries laboured their slow way up the incline that led to the heights.

'All right, Jumbo. Where's the fire?' the CO asked without any apparent sense of urgency. But then the CO had been soldiering so long, Digby-Watham told himself, that nothing alarmed him any more. Sometimes, the Major felt, the CO thought more of his horses than he did of human beings. Swiftly he filled the old colonel in with the latest information that Gore-Smythe had given him at the *Dom Hotel*.

The CO, took it very calmly, smoking his old pipe and sipping his coffee and rum, commenting only, 'Nervous Nellies those Intelligence chappies. Always have been. But carry on, Jumbo.'

Behind them the lorries had reached the summit and were quickening their pace as they headed for the Hussar's camp.

'Well, sir,' the Major continued, sweating now from the strong drink, despite the dawn coolness, 'If trouble really does come from the air, GHQ has decided we will have to protect ourselves.'

'Can't do much from a hoss against an aeroplane,' the CO said wrily. 'Though I once did see a stallion on heat do something very rude to an aeroplane, but it was parked, or whatever they call it, of course.' Then, for some reason, he puffed severely at his pipe.

Digby-Watham looked at the old man in some bewilderment, but he told himself that the CO was probably already senile – he did spend a lot of time poking under mares' tails at parades, completely ignoring the turnout of the troopers. He shrugged and got on with it. 'Brigadier Gore-Smythe has, how-ever, made some special provision for the eventuality that we are attacked from the air.' He finished his coffee and rum and rose to his feet, 'If you'd care to get up, sir, I shall show you.'

The CO frowned. 'Must I? I always like to finish my pipe in the morning before I start thinking. People think too much as it is. If everyone just sat down and smoked a pipe,' he added obscurely, 'the world would be a better place, Jumbo, believe you me.' Then he saw the look on the big major's face, shrugged and said, 'All right, if I must!'

Together they walked over to where the first of the lorries had come to stop, the troopers rising hastily to salute the CO, but he didn't seem to notice, though immediately he saw one of the horses loosing a stream of hot droppings onto the ground he barked, 'Don't like the look of that shit, McCarthy. Something wrong with his guts. Watch his bowels for the next few days.'

Behind him McCarthy put his finger to his forehead and whispered to his pal, Trooper Kerrigan, 'Poor old bugger. He's gone looney at bloody last.'

They paused at the first lorry as the begoggled driver got down from his open cab and sprang to attention. 'Well?' the CO urged. 'Let's get on with it, Jumbo.'

'Sir.' Digby-Watham nodded to the driver, who wore the cannon badge of the Royal Artillery.

Hastily, he went to the back of the lorry and untied the rope which held the canvas down.

The CO stared blankly as the gleaming weapon, bolted to the floor of the vehicle, was revealed. 'I know it's some sort of gun,' he barked. 'But what kind?'

'Ack-ack,' the Major said proudly, as if he had invented it personally, 'A new quick-firer

251

which we've just bought from the Swiss.'

'Didn't know they made guns. Thought they only made chocolate and those bloody irritating cuckoo clocks!'

'Well, they do, sir, and we've got three of them.'

'But who's going to fire 'em? My Hussars don't know anything about popguns like that!'

'Two lorryloads of gunners, sir. All been trained in these new anti-aircraft guns, sir.'

'Hope they don't frighten the hosses,' the CO said sourly. 'Ah, well, suppose we'd better get on with it. Tell the adjutant to have the men ready for 0700 hours. I'll just finish my pipe in peace.' With that the CO turned, silver spurs clanking on his spindly legs, and staggered back to his stool.

On the opposite height the civilian in the shabby suit would have dearly liked to have known what was in the newly arrived lorries, but the distance was too great and the canvas concealed the contents. All the same, he reasoned, the chief would like to know about them. Hastily he sprang on his battered bike and started to freewheel down the hairpin vineyard road to the gleaming snake of the Moselle so far below.

All was hectic activity this September morning at the little former Imperial German air strip beneath the great shadow of Limburg Castle. Mechanics hurried back and forth fuelling up the ancient biplanes. Others checked the engines. A low tractor towed the bombs which would be linked to the attachments that had been fitted secretly the previous evening in the hangars away from prying civilian eyes. There was an almost wartime urgency about the field which made the chief mechanic remark cheerfully, 'We'll be putting the shitdogs behind bars up there again, if it goes on like this.' He indicated the castle which had been a prisoner-of-war camp for allied prisoners during the war.

In the mess the pilots were unusually sober, for them. Before their performances in America they had always drunk heavily, although they knew how dangerous it was to do so and fly. But the shame of their existence, performing to smalltown hicks, had made them do so. Now they knew they had to keep sober; their mission was far too important for them to fail just because they had been hitting the bottle.

Even young von Einem, generally regarded as the clown of the Hell's Angels, was unusually serious as he ate his bread and sausage from the wooden board which served as a plate. This morning there were no comments about the 'Condemned man ate a hearty breakfast,' though in reality he was a condemned man, but he didn't know that, of course. Instead his talk, like that of the others, was of tactics, just as it had been during the war, with, 'Come in low; when we're above the target we rise to commence the bombing...' and so on.

At eight, von Horn appeared in the little mess. He was worried at the latest news, but he didn't let them see that. He had something else up his sleeve if their mission failed. He nodded to *Haupmann* von Pritzwitz and the latter rapped his spoon against his cup for attention.

Von Horn cleared his throat in a self-important manner. '*Meinen Herren,* your target is the *alte Romerbrucke*' – the Roman bridge – at Trier.'

There was a slight gasp at that announcement and someone objected, 'We shall be risking German lives as well as those of the Tommies when they cross that bridge.'

Von Horn shook his head firmly. 'No, you won't. We have made special provision for that eventuality.' He looked around at their

254

serious, concerned faces.

'How?' someone asked.

'We have spread the rumour that the first Tommies coming, their cavalry, are a wild bunch. The *Trierer Volksfreund,* the local newspaper, has loyally assisted us. It has appealed for public calm and police assistance to help prevent an incident.' Von Horn gave them a crooked smile. Naturally the police who are working for us are only too eager to oblige. As soon as the first Tommy outriders are spotted by the police at a spot some seven kilometres north of the city heading for it, the whole of central Trier *including the Romerbrucke,* will be sealed off from all German civilians. When you attack, the only people in the area will be the Tommies. It's up to you, *meinen Herren,* not to overshoot.'

'We won't,' *Hauptmann* von Pritzwitz said firmly, giving his pilots a severe warning stare.

'All we need is the bridge destroyed,' von Horn continued, 'and several score Tommies killed. They tell me many of them are Irishmen – one of the many wild races they have over there, though they don't wear skirts like some of them and blow into pigs' bladders. It will be good for propaganda if some of these wild men are killed. We can say that they died fighting England's battles.' He shrugged. 'But that is just a minor thing. The main thing is that Germany is rallied by a blow struck for our national unity and freedom.'

There was a murmur of agreement from his attentive audience. Von Einem said, 'We'll show the damned Tommies, never fear! We didn't do too bad in the last show. We'll do even better this time.'

Von Pritzwitz beamed. 'Well said, von Einem!' he commented.

Von Horn raised his hand for silence, looking around at their keen faces, knowing that one way or another they would have to die once they had carried out their task; they were too much of a liability. They knew too much. 'Gentlemen, I would like to wish you all *Hals und Beinbruch.*'*

'Hals and Beinbruch!' they echoed as one.

Von Horn raised his hand in salute. Knowing it was time to go, they rose and began to button up their leather flying jackets, reaching for their helmets and goggles.

*Literally 'Break your neck and leg'. The equivalent of the English phrase 'Happy landings'.

256

Outside, the mechanics swung the propellers of the waiting Sopwith Camels. One by one their engines burst into life as the crew chief in the cockpit switched on. They were ready to go.

Chapter Eight

'A Squadron will advance, *at the walk!*' the squadron leader ordered, rising in his stirrups to issue the command. 'Bags o' swank, lads! Remember who you are, the King's Royal Irish Hussars.' They had come down from the heights now and were on the narrow riverbank road which led to Trier, the outline of the two cathedrals already visible to the left of the Moselle.

Hidden in the first of the anti-aircraft lorries, Major Digby-Watham waved at the others behind them to prepare for trouble. The gunners of the Royal Artillery, mostly old sweats who had fought in the Great War, raised their thumbs to indicate that they had spotted the signal.

In front of A Squadron, walking their horses down the dusty country road between medieval half-timbered houses which for some reason had their wooden shutters tightly closed, there was nobody to be seen. Indeed, as one of A Squadron's troopers remarked after their major's command, 'By the Holy Mother of Jasus, who are we gonna swank to, Paddy? There's never a soul about.' The country road was completely deserted.

Still as A Squadron led the way into Trier, the mounted band struck up an Irish jig, and the look of bewilderment on some of the troopers' faces vanished as they enjoyed the old music of their homeland, the Emerald Isle.

In the middle of the column, the old senile colonel busied himself with staring at the mares' rumps and looking hard at any droppings that the horses in front of him made, the danger that Major Digby-Watham had pointed out completely forgotten. He told himself he had survived the Boer War, the Great War, the March on Baghdad. He'd survive the crossing of this German river, whatever it was called. He concentrated on the horses' rumps...

A mile away, the crew of the *Swordfish* crouched in readiness beneath the huge tarpaulin which now covered the craft, one that bore the fading legend *'MOSEL SCHIFFAHRT G.M.B.H.'* Just before it had grown light, Smith had somehow wedged the *Swordfish* between two of the pleasure steamers that had been laid up for the winter. It had been just in time. Thirty minutes later, a police patrol on horses had come cantering slowly down the towpath next to the steamers, obviously looking for the *Swordfish*. An hour later they had spotted a foot patrol as well. Still their luck had held and they had not been discovered.

Now everything in the centre of Trier was strangely quiet. Indeed there was a strange, brooding air about what should have normally been a busy place, and it was disquieting. Even McIntyre, not an imaginative man by any means, remarked upon it, saying, 'They're up to something.' He peered from beneath the tarpaulin. 'Not a soul in sight. Look.'

The others agreed and CPO Ferguson said, 'Ay, I think we're in for a wee spot o' trouble before long.'

Now in the far distance they could hear the faint strains of a brass band and Common Smith said sharply 'Stand by! This'll be them. The Eighth Hussars.

They're playing "Phil, the Fluter's Ball". It's got to be the Micks, hasn't it?'

'Bluidy Irish!' Ferguson intoned in his usual sour manner. 'Yon lot is all bluidy Papists!'

At any other time they would have laughed at the grizzled old Scot – he seemed to hate everyone. But not now. The situation was too tense. They all knew that the trouble would commence soon and if they didn't play their part effectively the consequences could be disastrous, not just for a few soldiers, but perhaps for the whole of Western Europe.

Smith squirmed round to where Dickie Bird lay. 'Get to the bridge, Dickie, see if everything's all right. Chiefie, see that the engine-room people move back. You, deck watch, stay here for the time being.' Trying to make as little noise as possible, the men involved moved away under the canvas, covered by the two large pleasure steamers, one on each side of the *Swordfish*.

The strident blare of the brass band grew ever louder, accompanied by the clip-clop of many hooves on the cobbles of the road leading towards the ancient Roman bridge. Then Smith heard something, the faint drone of aircraft engines. He flashed a look at McIntyre, who nodded and snapped, 'You can betchyer life it's them. The Hell's Angels.'

Common Smith made his decision, knowing that it was one that might well mean the end of the gallant *Swordfish* and her crew, for both banks of the Moselle here were in German hands. 'All right!' he cried, 'Raise anchor, take off the tarpaulin. We're going to that bridge, chaps.'

'Come hell or highwater!' Billy Bennett said enthusiastically.

Ginger Kerrigan looked at him contemptuously, 'Who the frig do you think you are, yer silly bugger, bloody Admiral Nelson?'

Now the *Swordfish* started to back out between the two white-painted pleasure boats, and the sounds of the band and the aeroplane motors grew ever louder.

At the bridge, Dickie Bird gave his orders as the crew doubled to their battle stations and an anxious Smith eyed the river to their front, knowing instinctively that von Horn would have more than one trick up his sleeve. The situation was too serious, too important, for him to fail now after all this planning. Next to him McIntyre pulled out his pistol and checked the magazine. 'They're not getting me alive, Smith,' he muttered grimly.

Common Smith nodded his agreement, saying, 'Don't worry, Major, we've beaten him before. We'll do it this–' He stopped abruptly and then cried, 'Look, here they come – The Hell's Angels!'

The horizon was peppered by nine black dots getting larger by the moment, as A Squadron of the Eighth Hussars prepared to cross the old Roman bridge.

'It's them all right!' McIntyre cried. 'You can see they mean trouble by the way they're coming in. Come in low and then rise to drop their bombs. Old-style tactic.'

Smith knew what he meant. If they came in too low and dropped their bombs they could possibly blow up their own planes as well.

As the Hussars crowded the far end of the bridge, cutting down the width of their formation to cross it, the lorries had halted. Men were fumbling with the canvas backs. Smith didn't know what they were about. His mind was concentrated on the advancing planes. He yelled, 'Ginger and Billy, get on to the Lewis gun. Draw a bead on them as soon as they're over the bridge and give 'em all you've got! Otherwise we've got a massacre on our hands.' He bent over to the voice-tube, whistled and ordered, 'Full ahead, both. *NOW!'*

The planes were getting bigger and bigger. At the far end of the bridge, the riders stared at them in some bewilderment. Major Digby-Watham yelled out and working all out the Royal Artillerymen swung up their weapons.

Now the Hell's Angels swung from side to side in their old classic wartime attack formation, as if they could expect opposition at any moment and were trying to outfox their opponents. Down below, Digby-Watham cursed, 'Stay bloody still!' he cried, enraged, as the gunners tried to home-in on their targets.

Von Einem was singing happily to himself. It was a song he had learned from his English governess, Miss Parkins, long before the war. It was the same bit of doggerel which he had always hummed to himself when he had gone into action during that 'war to end wars'. *Fie ... fi ... fo ... fum ... I smell the blood of an Englishman.'* His blue eyes gleamed excitedly behind the goggles attached to his leather flying helmet. Now the Hussars were close enough. Soon he would *smell* their blood! He pulled back the joystick and the old British fighter started to rise slowly, laden as it was with bombs.

Now at last the gunners were ready. The sergeant in charge yelled above the sudden shuffling and neighing of the horses, made nervous by the sound of the aircraft engines, 'Take aim – prepare to fire!'

Next to the old colonel, who had not yet seemed to have noticed anything unusual, his batman crossed himself and muttered, 'For what we are about to receive…' The CO looked at him in a slightly puzzled fashion and then concentrated on the problem of how they would get sufficient remounts once they were back in England now that the damned politicians in the new Irish Free State were proving to be so awkward.

Flying higher than the rest of the Hell's Angels, *Hauptmann* von Pritzwitz knew that they were now at the best bombing height. He pushed his stick forward and flashed ahead of the formation. As he passed through their planes he signalled downwards. They knew what that meant – go into the attack. Each pilot grasped the toggles which would release the bombs attached to the plane's wings.

Digby-Watham tensed. In front of him the Hussars of A Squadron crowded together, uncertain of what to do next. Should they go forward or should they stay where they were? Either way they were a prime target, confined to the narrow approach road and the equally narrow Roman bridge. If the gunners didn't stop the Germans now there would be hell to pay, especially as the whole Regiment was piling up behind the stalled A Squadron.

Von Einem waved out of his open cockpit to right and left. The other two pilots of his flight knew what to do. Von Einem was going to go in for the attack. They grinned and grinned back, telling himself that this was like the old days when they had been young and carefree, not giving a damn whether they lived or died. 'Just let me make a handsome corpse,' he thought to himself and then yelled to the others though he knew they couldn't possibly hear, *'March or croak, old friends!'* He pushed the joystick forward.

His little plane seemed to fall out of the blue sky and the land reared up to meet him. The thrill of the attack contorted his face wildly. The riders were milling around the bridge. He couldn't possibly miss. The Hell's Angels were going to do it! He gave himself another 50 metres. He glanced at the instruments, fingers prepared to release his bombs.

Suddenly he was startled to see cherry-red spurts of angry fire erupting from below. Black puffballs of smoke appeared to left and right of his aircraft. The little plane rocked wildly. He could hear the steel shrapnel tearing savagely at the canvas. 'What in three devil's names,' he began to curse, but he never finished it. The little plane staggered horribly and seemed to stop in mid-air. Frantically he worked at the stick and the rudder. There was no response, then the engine spluttered, started, coughed, stuttered and then terrifyingly stopped altogether.

Von Einem screamed. He had lost control. He felt his bladder evacuate, his crotch suddenly a hot, wet mess, as the shattered little Sopwith Camel fell out of the sky, turning and turning in a wild spin. For an instant he blacked out, then he came to. The ground was rushing up to meet him. He had no parachute. There was nothing he could do. He flung up his arms in one last futile gesture to cover his face and then it happened. The Sopwith Camel slammed into the side of the redstone cliff bordering the bridge, the bombs exploded and the plane disintegrated. Immediately the wreckage burst into flames. But by then von Einem was dead.

'Christ Almighty!' McIntyre exclaimed, as yet more of the anti-aircraft guns opened fire at the attacking planes. 'Didn't think this British Army had it in it to pull something like this out of the frigging hat!'

Common Smith laughed as above the bridge yet another of the attackers was hit and came tumbling out of the shell-pocked sky, its wings falling away from the fuselage. 'That's the stuff to give the troops!'

On the approach road, the regimental band had recovered from the shock of the sudden attack and under the directorship of a fat bandmaster was blaring out the Hussars' march, though Smith guessed no one could really hear it with the thump of the guns and the roar of the aircraft engines.

Watching the destruction of his Hell's Angels, *Hauptmann* von Pritzwitz was seized by a sudden blind rage. His was the only plane not weighed by bombs. Instead he had ordered the mechanics at Limburg to attach twin machine-guns to the engine cowling like they had done in the war when they had been a fighter squadron – bombing they had left to more pedestrian outfits. He

267

pushed the stick forward and came wheeling downwards at well over 150 kilometres an hour, eyes narrowed against the howling wind, squinting the best he could through the gunsights.

The ground rose up to meet him. Puffs of smoke exploded all about the plane. But he seemed to bear a charmed life as he dived for the guns. Now he could see the figures of the gunners quite clearly as some ran for more shells for their quick-firers. 'Arseholes!' he snarled, his face contorted into a sneer. He reached for the trigger of the twin machine-guns and pressed it. Tracer spat from the muzzles. The bullets splattered the road. He could see blue sparks erupting from the cobbles. Men went down, shells falling from their arms as they slammed to the ground. But there were others. Now the gunners were concentrating on the lone plane, homing in on him.

It was as if he were flying through a black-red network of exploding flak shells. Shrapnel ripped the length of his plane. Still he pressed home his savage attack, as yet another of his Hell's Angels fell from the sky trailing smoke behind it, to plunge straight into the Moselle in a great burst of angry white water.

Then it happened. He gave a great gasp as the shell splinter sliced off the end of his prop and ricocheted straight for him. He had no time to duck. The red-hot metal hit him in the centre of his face. It was as if someone had thrust a red-hot poker at him. Then a black veil descended and he knew no more as he fell out of the burning sky.

Chapter Nine

Up on the opposite hilltop the signaller watched as the last flight came winging in in one last, desperate attempt to destroy the bridge and the riders now on it. They waved from side to side like the battle aces they had once been in the war. But then they had faced slow-shot old-fashioned artillery, hastily adapted to the new anti-aircraft role. Now they were being confronted by the latest Swiss flak guns which could fire 20mm shells at a tremendous rate.

Shells whizzed up to meet the attack. To the operator crouched over his morse key, ready to signal the outcome of the attack to von Horn in Limberg, it seemed they were flying into a solid wall of sudden death.

On the ground the sweating artillerymen slammed home magazine after magazine into the breeches of their weapons, urged on by a near frantic Major Digby-Watham. On all sides the cobbles were littered with gleaming, steaming brass shell-cases. Still the Hell's Angels came on, intent on carrying out their vital mission and avenging their comrades of so many years who had already been shot down.

'Brave buggers,' McIntyre commented in his hard-bitten way as the *Swordfish* drew ever closer to the old Roman bridge. 'Still, knock them out of the friggin' sky. *Soon!*'

Common Smith agreed. Now there seemed to be about 500 Hussars on the bridge, strung out in a loose formation. If the bridge were hit now they wouldn't stand a chance, the troopers and their mounts would go hurling to their deaths in the Moselle below. He flung up his glasses. One of the three attacking planes had been hit. It was trailing black smoke flecked with angry cherry-red flames. Still the pilot kept his machine in the air, desperately fighting to keep on course. And Smith could guess why. He was going to crash the Sopwith Camel onto the bridge in a last suicidal attempt to destroy it.

'Ginger!' he yelled, 'Get that plane – the one with smoke coming from it.'

Ginger Kerrigan needed no further instructions. He too had guessed the intentions of the pilot of the stricken plane. He flung up his Lewis gun, pressed the big butt into his shoulder and opened fire. Tracer sped upwards in a lethal arc, in the very instant that another of the attackers was hit, staggering as if it had suddenly run into a brick wall and then fell out of the sky, Ginger's vicious burst ripped into the suicide plane.

The German pilot didn't stand a chance. A wing was ripped off and began to float downwards, fluttering like a leaf. The engine stopped, thick smoke pouring from it. The pilot rose from his seat. Watching through his glasses, Common Smith could visualize the German's horror at this moment. What was he going to do? Should he chance trying to jump – he had no parachute – or should be attempt to land the plane and perhaps save himself?

Ginger Kerrigan made that decision for him. Deliberately, he aimed at the fixed undercarriage, ripping off another vicious burst. The struts splintered. A wheel tumbled out of the sky. Now the pilot's last chance of saving himself was gone. Smith watched as the pilot sat back in the shattered cockpit with his arms folded across his white flying suit, resigned to his fate. A moment later the battered, crippled plane smashed into the ground and disintegrated into a thousand pieces.

That was enough for the pilot of the third plane. He swung the Sopwith around in a tight turn, followed by an angry salvo of 20mm shells from the ground. Soon, the Sopwith was a black dot on the horizon.

Common Smith breathed a sigh of relief. At long last it was all over. The great German revenge attack, which might well have rallied the nation behind the nationalists who would have laid the foundations for a second world war, had failed. Then something caught his eye. Through his glasses he glimpsed a figure on the hilltop opposite. He looked suspicious. 'Dickie!' he called urgently.

'What is it, old bean?' his shipmate asked cheerfully, obviously relieved, too, that the threat was over.

'Up there. On that rise. What do you make of that civilian?'

Hastily Dickie flung his glasses and

focussed them on the person who was crouched over a box, while behind him another civilian came into view, a pair of earphones held close to his head, as he obviously tried to cut out the clatter of the cavalry and the blare of their band as the regiment of Hussars began to cross the Moselle bridge. 'I don't know exactly,' he answered hesitantly. 'But could it be a – a detonator box, do you think?'

'*WHAT?*' Common Smith exploded.

'Christ all-bloody mighty!' McIntyre yelled in sudden alarm. 'You're right! That bugger von Horn has out-foxed us after all. The guy with the earphones is some sort of signaller. He's taking his orders from von Horn, I'll bet my bottom dollar on it. Now the air attack has failed they're going to blow the bridge. That bastard von Horn had it planned like this all the friggin' time.'

Desperately, frantically, Smith spun his glasses round from the hilltop, where the two civilians crouched, to the river bank and steep slope leading to the water. On the bridge the regimental band was happily playing 'Garry Owen' and some of the Hussars were whistling the old Irish jig or singing their own parody of it: 'Taties and fishes and all nice dishes.'

273

'There it is,' he yelled in sudden alarm.

'What?'

'A cable – can't you see it, leading off the bank and into the water?'

'What do you make of it, Smithie?' Dickie Bird cried.

'They've planted an explosive charge in the centre of the river, just in case our engineers have checked the chambers under the bridge itself.'

McIntyre opened his mouth to say something. Common Smith didn't give him a chance. Next moment he had flung himself out of the wheelhouse and was racing across the deck, scattering the men standing there watching the cavalry clatter past above. Hardly pausing to take a breath he flung himself over the side into the cold water of the Moselle and was striking out with the same speed that had won him the swimming cup at Dartmouth all those years before.

'Smithie!' Dickie Bird cried desperately, knowing that if the man on the hill detonated the charge now, Smith didn't stand a chance. But Smith wasn't listening. His whole being was concentrated on that black length of cable as he flashed through the water, his arms going like pistons.

Even as he swam furiously towards the

cable, he was planning what he was going to do. He would have to exert all his strength and hopefully pull out the lead that would prevent the submerged explosive from being detonated. *'Yes,'* a hard, cynical voice at the back of his mind rasped, *'if they don't explode it before you get there!'* He ignored the voice. He had to.

On the deck of the *Swordfish,* McIntyre watched helplessly, telling himself he knew why that supposedly languid young Englishman had won the VC back in 1918. It was because he was brave. Not far away Ginger Kerrigan, knowing that the skipper might well be swimming to his death, swung the Lewis gun to its farthest extent. He knew already he could not reach the German up there with the box. But he hoped he might well rattle him for a few vital moments. He pressed the trigger and a stream of slugs poured from the ugly muzzle of the Lewis gun, but the rounds fell short as he guessed they would. He could see the glowing slugs striking the stone in tiny flashes, perhaps a dozen yards away from the man with the box. But the sudden burst startled him. He ducked instinctively and took his hands off the detonator plunger. Ginger had given the skipper a few more minutes to live.

Desperately Smith swam on. A man appeared from the other side of the bridge. He had a pistol in his hand. Smith would have groaned if he'd had the strength to do so. The man shouted something in German, lifted the pistol and took aim. At that range he couldn't have missed. But again luck was on Smith's side. McIntyre saw the man, too. 'Bugger that for a game of soldiers!' he cried angrily and fired without seeming to aim. The German shrieked, high and hysterical like a woman. He threw up his hands and reeled backwards into the water.

On the hillside, the man with the detonator box had recovered from the shock of being fired at. Through his glasses Dickie could see how his heavy jaw set in a hard manner as he grasped the plunger once more. Next to him, McIntyre growled. 'That bastard von Horn had planned it like this all along. The Hell's Angels were a front. War heroes returning to pay back their debt of honour. They were expendable. Von Horn was going to blow the bridge right from the side whether they were successful or not.'

Dickie Bird wasn't listening. He stared through his binoculars at Smith going all out. He was nearly there, but would he beat the man with the detonator? His tension was now so great that the knuckles of his hands holding the glass turned white as he willed Smith to make it before it was too late.

Suddenly Smith stopped swimming. He'd grabbed hold of the black cable, treading water as he did so. On the *Swordfish*, Ginger Kerrigan loosed off another burst at the man with the detonator box. This time the angry volley didn't deter him. He had turned the key which set the mechanism in motion. Now he was going to trigger the electric charge which would set off the explosives hidden at the bottom of the Moselle.

McIntyre, feeling the sweat trickling down the small of his back unpleasantly, cried through gritted teeth, *'Come on, Smith! Come on, for fuck's sake!'* Above the spot where Smith grappled with the cable, the bridge was still crowded with Hussars, their tightly packed horses jostling each other. A tragedy was in the making if Smith didn't break the cable in a second or two.

Smith knew that too, as he desperately pulled at the cable with all his remaining strength, his chest heaving with the effort, as he tried to part out the unseen leads. The veins at his temples stood out and his face was contorted as he swore and cursed, praying for the leads to snap.

Suddenly he felt some leverage. Had he done it! He redoubled his efforts, crying through gritted teeth, *'Come on! Come one!'* In the same instant that the man on the hilltop pressed home the plunger, Smith felt the cable come loose. Then he fell backwards into the river water, gasping frantically like a man who had just run a great race and won. He had done it.

Now the Eighth Hussars started to leave the bridge, the sounds of their band echoing and re-echoing in the circle of hills, while Smith lay there in the shallows, all energy drained from him, and on the *Swordfish*, the men cried, 'Good show, Mr Smith! Well done, Mr Smith!' and waved frantically. For it was all over at last.

August 1942

The big heavy Canadian colonel was finding the climb heavy going, but he was determined to make the top of the cliff. Below more and more landing barges were grinding to a halt in the shingle of the beach. The Germans in Dieppe's strongpoints were pouring a tremendous fire at the running men of the Canadian division, going into combat for the first time. Men were falling on all sides. Still they pressed home their landing, as farther out to sea the heavy ships of the Royal Navy slammed shell after shell into the German positions.

But the British commando to which Colonel McIntyre was attached as special intelligence officer had found a fissure that sheltered them from enemy fire as they clambered up the heights on their scaling ropes. The Germans had previously attempted to block the gap with tangles of razor-sharp barbed wire, but tough young commandos had gone ahead of the main party and were busy snipping through the wire so that their comrades could follow. Here and there one of them would be hit by a German sniper, pitching to his death far below on the rocks of the beach.

Still they pressed on, with two young commandos helping a red-faced McIntyre when they came to a particularly tough spot. He resented their help, but he knew he was too old to be intolerant. So he let them aid him. Besides he knew all the effort was worthwhile. He had come to this embattled French port to kill a man: someone he would have dearly loved to have killed nearly 20 years before. Oh, yes, the effort was worth it all right!

Finally they breasted the cliff and lay gasping in the cropped grass. No one had stopped them. The Germans were concentrating their withering fire on the main body of infantry trying to come up from the beaches where the Churchill tanks the divisional commander had hoped would get them off the shoreline lay blazing, knocked out by concealed German anti-tank guns. McIntyre shook his head. It was like the same slaughter he had witnessed at Vimy Ridge in the last show when the fathers of these boys had been slaughtered, too, in massed frontal attacks.

'All right, chaps,' the young commando officer in charge of the party ordered above the snap-and-crack of the small arms fight and the thunderous boom of the heavy guns, 'there's their naval intelligence HQ. Let's go and take them out while we've still got a chance. I have an awful feeling that things are going awfully badly for the poor Canucks.'

The commandos needed no urging. They knew they would be discovered sooner or later. They surged forward in an extended line, bodies bent low like men fighting against a strong wind. They headed for the art nouveau building that had once been some rich Frenchman's summer villa and which they all recognized from the sand-table briefing.

'C' had briefed him, the new 'C', very upper class and old Etonian, 'Colonel, this chap of yours has sewn up the whole of the French Channel coast. He's got his spies, agents, informers everywhere. If we're ever going to invade France without too much difficulty, the head of that organization must be liquidated. These treacherous French must be shown that we British have a long arm and that we can hit their German masters when and wherever we like.' He had stared at McIntyre with those cold almost dead grey eyes of his and added, 'Colonel McIntyre, it will be your task to recognize him – you are the only one of us who can – *and then kill him!*'

McIntyre ran as best he could with the commandos, who were half his age, for the German naval intelligence HQ, remembering those words from Major General Sir Stewart Menzies.

Somewhere to their right a machine-gun began to rattle like an irate woodpecker. The nearest commando didn't hesitate. Even as he ran he lobbed a grenade into the German gun-pit. There was a vivial flash of angry red flame and a man was hurled out of the hole. He was followed a moment later by his severed, gory head which rolled away like an abandoned football.

They came to the door of the villa. A commando smashed the window to the right and flung in a grenade. Another slammed his booted foot against the door, which flew open in the same moment as the diversionary grenade exploded. The commando flung up his tommy-gun and sprayed a cruel burst from left to right inside, shouting excitedly, 'Try that on for size, mate!'

Then they were in, springing over the dead German sailor sprawled out in the hall in a pool of his own blood. An officer in the blue uniform of the *Kriesgsmarine* leaned over the stairway, pistol in hand. The young commando officer didn't give him a chance. He fired first. The officer came tumbling down the stairs, trailing blood behind him. They ran on.

A tough commando sergeant slammed his shoulder against the ornate door to his front. It swung open. They could hear the voices from inside, crying in panic, '*Nicht schiessen* – don't shoot.'

McIntyre pushed by the commando officer, breathing hard and telling himself he was getting too old for this kind of rough-house. 'Cover me, the Huns are a treacherous lot of baskets!' He burst into the room. At the far end there was a group of what were evidently staff officers, trying to keep out of the fighting. Indeed there was one of them cowering beneath the sand-table. Immediately their hands shot up above their heads when they saw the granite-faced Canadian with the big pistol in his hand.

All but one.

He stood there stonily, no emotion on his albino face with the painted-on eyebrows. The yellow skullcap of hair had vanished now to be replaced by a white cropped one. But there was no mistaking him. *'Von Horn! Admiral von Horn,'* McIntyre cried in triumph. He had found the man he had come to kill. *'Das sind Sie doch,'* he added.

The skinny German Admiral looked at him curiously, no fear on his lean, cruel face. 'I know you,' he said slowly, totally unconcerned by the sounds of battle outside and the enemy soldiers pouring into the big room.

McIntyre gave him his crooked grin. 'I

think you do. McIntyre is the name.'

For an instant there was a trace of fear on the Admiral's thin, almost emaciated, perverted face. '*You!* he choked.

'Yes, me!'

Von Horn reacted in a way that none of them expected, very fast for a middle-aged man. The grenade appeared as if by magic from behind his back.

'*Duck, for chrissake!*' the tough commando officer yelled frantically. His men flung themselves to the floor as the evil ball of metal packed with high explosive landed in the centre of the big room.

McIntyre was too slow.

Suddenly he was propelled off his feet, as if he had been struck by a gigantic fist. Something that felt like a red-hot poker bored its way into his guts. He moaned sadly, knowing already that he was finished. A black mist was threatening to envelop him. Vaguely he heard von Horn laugh and cry, 'We'll win in the end, McIntyre, you English are finished. We've beaten you here. You will never again land in Europe...'

McIntyre couldn't make out the rest of the words. They didn't matter. He had only one objective now. He tried to get his eyes to focus. Von Horn stood there, hands on his hips in the arrogant posture of the victor. 'Fuck you,' the Canadian said weakly, remembering those days so long before on the Moselle, and all the brave young men, long dead and gone. Instinctively almost, he pressed the trigger of his pistol. At that range, as he lay there dying, he couldn't miss. The impact at such short range lifted von Horn right off his feet. The bullet had hit his evil, cruel face. Now, as he fell, his features started to drip down to his chest like molten red sealing wax. It was then that they both died...

The old lady, who had once been very pretty but who had aged prematurely, sat in the rocking chair on the porch as the Canadian postman, looking grave and worried, walked down the drive to where he had parked his van near the coolness of Lake Ontario. She knew what the telegram contained. She hesitated. Then with trembling fingers, she forced herself to open it.

The prose was short and brutal in the style of the war. It read: *'Regret to inform you that your husband Lt. Col. D. McIntyre, DSO, MC has been killed in action. We shall forward you further details as soon as we have them.'* She read no more letting the telegram flutter out of her weak hand. 'He was really a good man,' she said to herself and then the woman, who had been once known as Fraulein Lena and had plied the Allied trains to Berlin as a whore, started to cry, softly and quietly. It was all over at last.

The publishers hope that this book has given you enjoyable reading. Large Print Books are especially designed to be as easy to see and hold as possible. If you wish a complete list of our books please ask at your local library or write directly to:

Magna Large Print Books
Magna House, Long Preston,
Skipton, North Yorkshire.
BD23 4ND